Duffle Bag Bitches 3

By

Alicia Howard

APR 17

CH

Duffle Bag Bitches 3

Chapter 1

The airport security officers are tripping out. They are thinking about nine eleven how many people lost their lives that day. Zane is thinking about Shannon, and how he can't live without her. As the smoke begin to clear, Zane looks up sees Nisha reaching for him. "Come on bruh. We only have a short time to get out of here." Nisha is trying to let him know that shit is not the way it seems.

"I can't leave my wife," he fussed.

"I would never leave your wife either. Shannon straight, trust me." Nisha needs this nigga on his feet. Time is running out.

Dizzy yells, "Zane come on nigga! We've got to get the hell out of here! They are on our ass." Zane runs, but he keeps looking back because he doesn't know where the hell Shannon is.

The three of them ran down the east terminal then ducked out a side door. They see the DBB's jet big as day. Zane is confused like a muthafucka, but it isn't the time to get the answers he wants. Dizzy got on first, then Zane, and Nisha. It is her job to make sure no one is left behind. Jay, Jasmine, and Shannon are on the jet already. "I can't live without him," Shannon cries.

"It's ok boo." Jay tries to calm her down.

A voice made all of them turn their heads. "You will never live without me as long as I can help it," Zane states.

Shannon jumps into his arms. "Baby I thought you were hurt! I didn't know what I was going to do without you. I can't imagine what life is like without you. The few months that I was mean to you killed me. The when I saw you at the meeting looking sexy, I said I'm getting my man back. Then that bitch called your phone." Shannon takes a breath. "You know I'm killing her right?" Shannon asked. Everyone on the jet burst out laughing at the amazing crazy love the two of them share.

"Girl you're not killing shit," Zane said then smiles kissing her.

"Anyway put me down, who is the bitch?" she asked punching him.

"Nobody!" Zane smiles taking a seat. Shannon fusses all the way back home. Zane laughs listen to her. He wouldn't want his life any other way besides with her crazy ass driving him crazy. Now that God has he blessed Zane with the family he never had. Soon Zane will have a crazy wife, best friend for life, a beautiful stepdaughter, and a new baby. He knows that it is time to go house shopping because Zane wants his family under one roof. His days of the bachelor pad life are over. He is glad about that too. He can't wait to get back tell Mack the great news. Shannon still doesn't know that Mack is alive. They have to go easy on her so that she wouldn't work the baby up too much.

Shannon is crazy enough already. She doesn't need Mack to add to the fire. Zane knows that Dallas will be in his feelings because he is going to ask Mack to be his best man. Shannon loves that crazy ass fool maybe because they are just alike. Zane has to laugh because he thought that Mack was sweet on Shannon. The two of them would have killed each other. Mack isn't checking for Shannon. He is too crazy to settle down. Zane looks around the jet even though Shannon is still in his ear bitching. All he can think about is how much he loves his life.

Chapter 2

Dallas is sitting in the new warehouse in the rehabilitation room with Mack as he works out. They are watching the news laughing at all the people that are talking to the reporters. It is funny how people that supposed to be in charge can get scared so fast when the shit hits the fan. "Man I would never hire a coward muthafucka like that to work for me," Mack states as he walks on the stair climber.

"Yeah, them pussies always bitching up when shit goes haywire. They're supposed to be trained to do that crap. You have to go through hell and hot water to get that job. I tried back in the day," Dallas told Mack.

"Nigga what the hell were you about to do up in there? Fool they would have fired your ass before they hired you," Mack teases him.

"That's what the fuck they did, but if their asses hired a nigga like me I would have gotten with them punk ass terrorists!" Dallas slap box the air.

"Man the terrorists would have fucked yo ass up!" Mack bust out laughing.

"Nigga stop playing with me." Dallas stuck his chest out because Mack is pissing him off testing his gangsta.

"Nigga get yo bitch ass on! Always in yo box ole fruity ass nigga."

Mack hopped off the stair master like he wasn't shot or in a coma a few weeks ago.

Dallas shakes his head at the nigga because this nigga is a certified soldier. He can get a pass any day to talk shit to Dallas the way he does. Dallas is about to talk some more shit, but his phone ring. His eyes grow wide when the name on the phone appeared. "Hey lovely," Dallas sing.

"Well hello stranger," she spoke in his ear.

"Why are you calling me?" Dallas asked. He doesn't get calls from her often.

"Well damn! I love you too." She laughs because she knows that she makes Dallas nervous.

"I love you more but why are you calling me." Dallas doesn't play any games.

"I'm calling as a hustler's mother. My oldest boy will be ready to take over the other end of the business world real soon," she informed him.

"Boss this is your world. I'm just a front nigga," Dallas said assuring her that he knows his place.

The son she speaks of is not hers biological. He is a kid she raised from the streets.

"You're the boss baby. I just an ole bitch that backs all this gangsta shit," she said with a laugh. Dallas loves this woman not only is she classy, but she is a G in every way.

"Well, send him to me when he ready to start. You know I've got his back, but our business is not the same," Dallas told her.

"I know that love. I know what line of work you're in don't sweat the small shit. I'm grateful to have you. Letting an ole bitch retire and shit." She is amazing to Dallas.

"I am here for whatever you want or need baby." Dallas got mack daddy on her.

"You're still trying to get this pussy boy? My husband will kill you and forgive me." She laughed but is deadly serious.

"I will pass on that then. You have already been good to me," Dallas thanked her.

"I see you love. Keep doing the good work. The bombs? Brilliant nice touch of class."

"I learned from the best," he told her.

"Yes, you did until next time." She ends the call with a kiss.

Mack walks back in the room with his dark chocolate body dripping with sweat. All that working out has his body rock hard. "Why in the hell are you smiling? Don't be in here playing with yourself and shit," Mack jokes.

"Nigga never! I just talked to the lady," Dallas stated, Mack's face changed.

"Is she coming here?" Mack is scared of her, not because of her gangsta, she fucks niggas up with her sex appeal.

"No. Not yet anyway. The lady son will be turning twenty-one next years. He has been groom since he a teenager to take over the drug trade." Dallas doesn't talk to many people about the lady, but Mack and Zane know who she is.

"Damn, that bitch has always been the truth in the Lou. I see she's not gonna let the name die for shit." The thought made Mack laugh.

Dallas looks at the cut up young nigga wanting to slap the shit out of him. "Man put your damn shirt on. Don't nobody want to see your body, fake ass Arnold Shawsnigga,

"Aye, nigga don't be mad cause I'm ripped up and shit. I'm not going to take your whores. At least not all of them," Mack talks shit slapping his rock hard abs.

"Take my bitches? You've got to get your money up first little nigga," Dallas boasts.

"My money is… Well yeah nigga, you got me there." They both broke out into laughter.

"My nigga, it's a blessing to have you back. The world was not the same without you," Dallas told him.

"You can thank God for the mistake of bringing me back." Mack is one silly ass dude sometimes.

"I thank God that he brought you back my nigga. I don't want to know what life is like without you. I had a taste of it, and it's not for me." Dallas holds his hand out. "My nigga for life the only capo that works the field," Dallas stated.

"For life! I told you I didn't want to be a capo," Mack said seriously.

"The lady told me you don't have a choice." Dallas breaks the news to him finally.

"Ain't that a bitch? She's just gonna pull a nigga out of the field because I got hit one time?" Mack is pissed.

"No. The said if you have a death wish and need to be out there doing it you can. You are and forever will be a Capo," Dallas schools him.

"Wait, I get the money and the action? Hell yeah! Let's do it." Mack is on cloud nine with that news.

Chapter 3

The jet settled down in the Lou at Lambert Airport. The crew is glad to be home safe and sound. They can go rest up spend time with their families. Until the payday meeting tomorrow at 3 p.m. They exit the jet with new things on their mind. Sometimes mission can wake you up to certain parts of your life. This mission did that for every member of the team.

Dizzy watched Shannon and Zane when they were on the jet. He missed that, and he believed that he would never find that again after his wife murder. Now he thinks that he will never find it because he closed that part of his heart off. He blames himself for them losing their lives. He is not at fault. Now that Ricks is dead, he feels free. No one is blackmailing him or driving him insane. Dizzy is free to do him that feels great. He is planning to live life to the fullest. The first thing he plans to do is move out of that damn dungeon.

Zane is all over the place with his feelings. He is about to be a father. Zane has never dreamed of having a wife or kids. Zane is about to have both. He never knew that a man like him could be so lucky, more so blessed. The way Zane has been over the years he wants to cry when Shannon told him that she is carrying his baby.

Zane has never loved anything more than Shannon. Zane is glad to be home so he can buy her a dream house that she can move into in a few weeks. Zane doesn't want to miss cravings, morning sickness, or the fussing that she will do.

He wants to be there for everything. Shannon brings joy to his life Zane is ready to do the same for her.

Nisha feels good that she was given the job to set off the bombs. She allowed her crew a chance to make a run for it. Kim the cop, that helped Dizzy has already put Dallas on the game. That the FBI was tipped off by a letter that Ricks left just in case, he didn't make it out alive. He had given up all the dirty on Zane and Dizzy that he could.

However, nothing that could hold up in court. Nisha knows she has been childish when she joined the family, and it is time for a change. She needs to get her place, stand on her two feet. Show the world that she is ready to be a woman, not a little girl. It is the only way she will get the respect she needs and wants

Jasmine is glad to be home. She is planning on letting Dallas know that she isn't going to be going on many missions. That is because Jasmine is about to lose her family watching her sister made her feel grateful. She has the man that she has in her corner.

Jasmine knows that she has been wrong and selfish but that is who Jasmine is, and that is hard to change. Jasmine doesn't know the price of beginning right comes with a huge loss sometimes. Only time will tell what kind of damage she has done. Jasmine is ready to weather the storm she made the bed. Now Jasmine must lay in it like a grown up.

Shannon has been afraid to tell Zane that she is pregnant because she was so mean to him. That was the reason Shannon called everything off, because she didn't know if she would keep the baby. It is hard taking care of one child alone. Shannon doesn't want to have to do it again.

She knows that Zane is not the type of man that would leave her hanging. The life they lived could claim their lives at any time that's what scared her.

The day he came to the meeting smelling and looking great then a bitch called him. Shannon knew then she would rather die with him than without him. Zane thought she was playing about killing the bitch. If Shannon ever finds out who the bitch is, that bitch is a done dollar. For the moment, Shannon is cool because she has her baby back.

Jay is glad to be home. She is pleased that she has someone special in her life. Jay called Q to let him know that she would be touching down soon. Q told her that he would be there waiting for her. That man loves her. Jay smiles as she walked into the airport spotting Q holding an "I love you Jay" sign.

He is so sweet and silly at times. Jay loves him back. She knows that he will be the man she marries one day. There is much about her life that

Jay wants to change. Jay got a funny feeling that someone is watching her as she hugs and kiss Q.

That made her remember that it's a must find out who the stalker is. Jay has to because she isn't going to be able to rest until she deals with that. For the time being, Jay is stressed and needs to release. Q is just what the doctor ordered to make her feel better. Jay gave him a sexy look and kissing him passionately.

He knows that she is looking for something to smoke on and get her poke on. That's cool with Q that is the reason Jay won his heart. She is more like his friend than his woman. A man can't ask for more than that in their lifetime. Nothing and no one going to take Jay from him.

Chapter 4

Mack has been back at his crib for a week or two now. It feels strange at times, and he keeps having dreams about the night he got shot. Then to top shit off this bitch, Mack hasn't talked to in months, is blowing him up like crazy.

The first time that he has fallen asleep, he awoke by the ringing of his phone. He looks at the number wanting to throw the phone across the damn room, but he isn't into wasting money even though he has it.

"What Tasha?" Mack is sleepy as hell.

"Hey, baby! I have been calling you like crazy!" She all happy and shit.

"Didn't they tell you I was dead?" Mack asked her.

"Yeah," Tasha's crazy ass replies.

"So why are you calling a fucking dead man," Mack yells.

"Because I know that it wasn't true. It is just your friend wanting to be mean to me because I love you so much," Tasha rambles.

"You don't love me. You love this dick girl." Mack chuckles to himself thinking it has been a while since he has some pussy.

"I love you not your dick. That's your ego thinking it's all about the dick. But it's really about you Mack." Tasha does love him.

"Tasha you don't want me. I am not shit for real and one day I'm going to die in these streets someday. Baby go find you a guy that's sweet and kind." Tasha is a good girl; a little naïve, but a great girl and her pussy grade A too.

Tasha begins to cry. He knew that she would start that shit. That is what he hates about her ass. "Tasha please stop crying, or I will hang up." Mack is a G, but he can't stand for a woman to cry.

"Ok, I will stop. I just want to be around you and lay with you. I can't sleep, Mack!" She cries some more.

"Where are you?" he asked.

Tasha is quiet too long. "Where are you?" Mack asked again.

"Outside your door," she whined. Mack knew that; she did this shit all the time.

Mack hangs up, walking to the door, and opening it. There stand Tasha; honey brown and five foot two. Two hundred pounds of sexy all in the right places and even amounts of breast and ass. She had long honey blonde quick weave and hazel green eyes. She wore a Seven tank top and jeans that hugged her ass just right. The bitch is bad. He doesn't remember her being that bad or thick because she is so damn clingy.

She smiled with tears in her eyes. "I missed you, Mack." Then she blushes looking at the floor. He grabbed her by the hand and led her to the bedroom. "I'm sleepy so can we sleep and talk in the morning?" Mack asked.

"Yeah." Tasha is just glad to be near his crazy sexy ass.

Mack's body is rock hard, and he sleeps naked. The same way he answered the door. Mack doesn't allow women to get in his bed with clothing. Tasha knows cause few times she has been there. Tasha strips down slipping into bed with him. Tasha can feel his manhood awaken as it presses against her ass.

"If you want to fuck we can." Tasha isn't really in the mood, but she said that because in the past when she told niggas that she doesn't feel like it, they would get mad.

"Baby don't pay that nigga down there no mind. Mack Jr is just talking shit, but I'm sleepy so cuddle with me love," Mack told her. She feels like she won the lottery.

"Ok daddy." Tasha kisses him snuggles close until sleep overtook them.

Dallas sat in the office of his condo smoking a Cuban and getting his dick sucked. He is in a perfect place because he has saved each member of his team a half a million apiece. Due to all the things he has been investing. At the day's meeting, the payout will be one hundred fifty thousand dollars each.

Dallas knows that will keep them straight. The bitch that is sucking his dick on him like a Hoover vacuum cleaner, but it just isn't working. Dallas is caught up on the boss calling and his last mission. That is something that he has to tell the team as well.

Dallas is about to end the setup allowing the working girls to increase their income. No one wants to be a hoe for the rest of their life. Dallas isn't about to be a pimp for the rest of his life. Dallas wants children someday, and he would never be able to explain to his daughter how or why he is a pimp. Dallas looks down at Kelly's thick chocolate slender frame.

Kelly stands five-foot-eleven, jet-black hair that naturally hang to the middle of her back. She should be ripping the runway not down on her knees pleasing Dallas. Kelly is the only one of his working girls that he fucks with like that. She is his bottom bitch, and she even knows it.

Kelly money is always triple what the other girls make. Tricks don't mind her upping the price because she is that cold. Kelly could have kept the extra cheese, but she never does. She always brings it home to daddy proudly. "Kelly baby go take a bath wait for me in bed."

Kelly's dark brown eyes stare at him. "Daddy I'm sorry I didn't make you cum the way you like too. I have to work hard on my skill." Kelly is still on her knees lowering her eyes to the floor because she feels she let him down.

"Your skills are at an all-time high. It's just daddy's got so much on his mind." Dallas was feeling some way about her right then. Kelly never complains even when Dallas curse her out or treat her badly for no reason. That is just the bull in him from time to time, but Kelly always understanding of what Dallas face daily.

"Yes, I know that. You have a hard job, and that's why I want to bring joy to it." Kelly got up to head to the bedroom.

"You do baby; you do," Dallas assures her she walks out of the office smiling. Kelly loves that man but never told him because she doesn't think he values her that much due to her job.

Chapter 5

Dizzy is up bright and early the next morning. He has an appointment with a real estate agent named Tequila. She is going to help him pick him a new condo out. Dizzy is scared to look for a house alone. He hasn't picked a home since he lost his family. It is time to live, so he plans to try to do just that.

He is not sure where he wants to start outside of moving. Dizzy thinks once he moves he will step his way into dating. Hell, he better go out and buy a few flick because he has not put it down in years. Of course, here and there he had some pussy he is a man. Now that is playing for keeps it time to brush up on his skills.

Dizzy has an all-black Range Rover that no one knows he owns because he never drives it anywhere. That is about to change he jumped in the ride confused for a minute because he is still getting acquainted with the car. However, it doesn't take long for him to get the hang of things. Dizzy riding in style today as he looks for his new home.

He whips into the lot jump out of the ride. Dizzy is feeling great. He stands in front of the Fenton Condos looking at the beautiful scenery. He likes it because it is bright and lovely. His wife would have loved the outside. That alone that gives him a great feeling about the place.

Those thoughts are broke when a thin caramel brown honey in a white collared blouse that hugs her shapely breasts. Along with a pin-stripe pencil skirt that hugs her small hips that seem huge for such a small framed woman approaches him. "Excuse me are you Delvin Thomas?" She knows his government name, so she has to be the lady he is there to see.

Her hair is in a jet-black bob with honey tips, and she has dark brown eyes. "Why, who wants to know?" Dizzy asked. He realized the thug has taken over him.

"Me sir. I am Tequila, your real estate agent." She smiles at him because she loves the roughness she getting from him.

"My bad baby. I'm Delvin love, pleased to meet you." He got his shit together and responded.

"The pleasure is all mine," Tequila assures him.

"Yes, it could be." He is flirting now. Dizzy doesn't know what is wrong with him. "Forgive me, love, I'm just on cloud nine today," he apologizes.

"No, it's quite flattering. Do you want to follow me?" she asked as she walks to the condos.

"I will follow you across the world love." Dizzy done it again. It caused him to laugh at himself, and she laughed too.

They entered a fantastic place. Dizzy feels like someone has just turned the lights on in his world as he listens to Tequila talk about the condo. This condo a two bedroom, two baths; it has a large master bedroom with a master bath and walk-in closet. There is a spacious second bedroom with two closets and vanity/desk in between them. The living room has French doors to the patio. The kitchen also includes a dishwasher, stove, microwave, refrigerator and a full-size washer & dryer. Does this sound like something that would work for your family?" she asked.

"I have no family love. It's just me, and I think this will be a great start. How much is it?" Dizzy asked.

"Fifteen hundred a month." She hates telling folks the price because most hightailed it out of there.

"Cool, I will be paying the rent up for the next two years. That's how long the lease is right?" Dizzy asked her.

"Yeah it is, but you don't have to pay all that at one time." Tequila is amazed by him.

"I know baby, but I'm a busy man. I am in and out of town, so I like to get small shit out of the way so I can enjoy my life." Dizzy hasn't experienced life in a while, but he plans to soon.

"I agree. Let's go do the paperwork." She has to get the man away from her. Dizzy is making her panties wet.

"Let's." He holds the door open for her.

Chapter 6

"Ugh, I wonder what my life would be like if I had no phone. What is it?" Zane said into the phone.

"Yo ass wouldn't have the fly-ass crib, bad ass ride, huge bank account, and soon to be sexy ass wife," Dallas states.

"Nigga shut yo punk ass up. What the hell do you want now?" Zane laughed at his partner.

"It's payday, my nigga. Meeting at three, you know what to do family," Dallas informed him.

"It's already one thirty. Why the fuck are you just now calling? Nigga, you're slipping," Zane fussed.

"Nigga I texted your sleepy ass two hours ago. Got no response, so I know your ass is still in fucking bed," Dallas schools him.

"Damn the baby already fucking with my body," Zane stated.

"Baby? What baby nigga?" Dallas is excited and shock at the same time. He hasn't seen a child in years. Dallas never let his girls get pregnant. That is bad for business. The last one that did he turned her ass loose. Then on out he has a set date that all the girls came to the office to get their Depo shots.

"I will tell you at the meeting. I don't have much time to talk now. In a minute. You know I have to pick up Dizzy's crazy ass." Zane is press for time.

"No doubt son in a moment." Dallas disconnects the call.

Zane rolls over, and the spot next to him is empty. Shannon has gone home to be with her daughter. All that shit is about to change. His family is about to be in the same house after the meeting today. He needs to watch Shannon's wild pregnant ass anyway. "Hello?" Shannon was sleepy and had an attitude.

"What's good fat mama?" That is going to be the nickname Zane call her all through this pregnancy.

"Boy don't call here with that bullshit." Shannon is in bitch mode.

"Oh shit, and it begins. Baby cool down; we have to meet Dallas at three," Zane told her as he sits naked on the edge of his bed.

"Oh fuck me in the ass! Let me get off this fucking phone, call the bitches, and get dressed to ride out," Shannon fussed some more. The baby had her too tired.

"I will text you the new location boo and try to be gentle love." Zane is worried about her.

"Boy bye." Shannon hung up.

"I love you too fat mama." He knows that the pregnancy was going to be a task. The beautiful baby, in the end, is worth the pain and suffering that Zane about to endure.

Dizzy is leaving the condo with the keys to his new place feeling like a boss. Tequila has offered to have a moving company pack his things, but he turned her offer down. He told her that he wants all new shit, and what is in his crib will be left in his old place for his landlord to do as he pleased with it.

She is in love with the strange man but stuck firm to her job. As Dizzy is leaving his phone, begin to ring. "Excuse me I have to take this call," he says her. She smiles nodding her head watching him.

"What's hood, my nigga?" Dizzy spoke coolly.

"Chillin Chillin." Zane is wondering if he had dialed the right number.

"That's Gucci nigga. What did I do for the honor of this call fam?" Dizzy is in rare form.

"It's payday, and we're meeting at the new spot. I'm in traffic about to come get yo smooth ass." Zane laughed, but he likes this look on his boy.

"Oh no son, just send me the info. I am driving myself," Dizzy told him.

"You doing what? Really? Ok cool." Zane hangs up thinking this nigga has popped a molly. It made him smile to see his friend is letting his nuts swing.

Dizzy ends the call to look over at Tequila giving him a funny look. "I'm sorry. I'm all off in your shit being rude. Forgive me; it's just a little business love." He is GQ for real that day.

"No, it's ok. You seem to be a very busy man. I understand, we are all done sir," Tequila told him.

"Great, I will be back here later today. Don't call me sir either. I'm not your father, but you can call me daddy," Dizzy says chuckling because he is acting up again.

"Well, you have a beautiful day dad." She passed him a business card with all her numbers on it hoping he will call.

"Baby that is rude of me. You don't have to call me Daddy," Dizzy apologized to the sexy lady.

"I don't mind," Tequila flirts with him.

He looks at her exiting the offices. That caused her to laugh. Dizzy is shocked that the woman is flirting with him too, but he will have to get to know her at another time. Duty calls.

Chapter 7

The crew pulled up to the new warehouse, and it was off the meter. Shannon, Jay, Jasmine, and Nisha were already in the office. Zane and Dizzy walk in talking shit with each other. Dizzy is telling Zane about the new crib and new bitch he is about to bag. Zane is tickled beyond words because the man has been reborn. It looks like he is going to be a monster.

The women are all chattering when they spot Dizzy. They all rub their eyes as if they were seeing the nigga for the first time in their lives. Jasmine has to speak on it, "Dizzy nigga you think you the shit or something?" They have become great friends over the past few weeks.

"No baby, you think I'm the shit." He kisses her on the lips.

"Boy are you crazy? I am married," she yells.

"I bet your pussy is saying something else." Dizzy smiles. He can't believe he said that but it is too late now.

Jasmine rolls her eyes walking away because she knows that he is right. Her pussy got wet once the sexy nigga walked in, and the kiss causes the juices flow.

"Boy you better leave my sister alone," Shannon said with a laugh.

"Girl hush, Zane sew that up so good he put a baby in it," Dizzy stated. Shannon waves him off.

"A baby what?" Dallas knows the bare minimal about it. He feels this shit will make it hard for Zane to let Shannon do her job.

"Yes sir, she is pregnant, that means that she will sit out the next mission." Zane looks at Dallas to let him know that he is dead ass serious.

"I never said that," Shannon stated.

Zane looks at her like she has bumped her damn head somewhere. "I just said it. You don't have to say shit. I did already you're about to be my wife. That's my baby you're carrying, so that is all that needs to be said." He looks at her. Shannon got her ass somewhere and sat down.

Nisha teases, "Damn I need a nigga like that." The whole room busts out laughing. Shannon knows when to hold and fold with Zane. He let her get her way, but if he is serious, she knows that there is nothing she can do but follow orders.

Dallas chime, "I want to thank you all for doing a great job in New York. That brings me to say that we never planned on doing this for the rest of our lives. We have made an enormous amount of money. I want you all to know that we're going to Vegas." The room went wild. Shannon is pissed because she knows that she will be at home for that one.

Dallas continues, "I'm glad that you all happy. We're about the hit this nigga Don Q. He owns a casino and a few strip clubs, but we're after the casino chips this go around. I also hate to inform you that this is the last mission that we will be doing. After this, we can go on and live healthy lives." Everyone in the room wondered what the hell normal was because none of them had ever had a normal life.

"So just like that, it's over?" Zane asked.

"Yeah you will be a Capo this go around so you will be able to be at home with your family," Dallas told him in a sad tone. Even though he is ending it all, he doesn't know what he is going to with himself. He has no one to love him. It is just him, whores, and money.

"Damn what I am gonna do with my life now?" Dizzy asks out loud because he has no one either.

Nisha feels the same way the men did, but she didn't let it be known. She doesn't want to look bad, so she just sucked it up. Shannon has Zane now, but she still needs the drive of doing dirt in her life. She wouldn't dare speak on it in her condition because Zane is not having that shit at all.

Jay is cool with that, but she has to kill the stalker that is following her around. If she doesn't, she will never be free from the bullshit that life can bring you when you live a certain way.

The next voice causes the whole room to freeze. "What the fuck you mean we out? What's a nigga like me going to do? What the hell is normal?" Mack fussed. Dallas shakes his head because that fool is not supposed to come out until he is called.

Shannon jumped out of her seat ran over to him. "You died! I saw it with my own eyes," she cries because she thinks she is dreaming.

"Sister I had my personal rescue team following me. They got me out of the car the moment you all pulled off, then the car blew up. I was in a coma for three months. A few people in this room know that I was alive because Roc brought them to the hospital where I was," he said as he holds her while she cried. Zane doesn't mind because he knows that it is family love that they shared.

"Shannon calm down. You're carrying my brother's baby. Soon to be his wife so no stress on that beautiful face ok." Mack is a man in every way. Nisha has never known how sexy he was up until now.

Zane is sitting in a plush chair; Shannon walks over to him. He holds his arms open, and she crawls up into his lap like she is a newborn baby. Zane loves this woman with his soul, and he spoils her no matter who is watching.

"Bruh we can't do this forever my nigga, and we have women on this team now. Jasmine is married, and her husband stays on my ass. The only reason I am not put the nigga to sleep because I will have to kill them both. Shannon is pregnant and about to be Zane's wife. You know how he is, look!" Dallas points to them all cuddled up, and that causes Mack to shake his head.

"What about you two?" Mack asked Nisha and Jay.

"I got a man, but he knows nothing. He won't stop my hustle," Jay informed him.

"I am trying to get me together, so niggas are not a factor at this time for me," Nisha let him know that nothing will stand in her way.

Chapter 8

"Dallas see we're all not in love. Unless you are calling it quits because you fell for a bitch, everyone doesn't want that square love that Zane's got," Mack barked.

"Nigga this not about square love. Don't disrespect me in my place of business. I am just thinking about someone other than myself. We're not going to need the money so what's the point? I will still have my whores out there getting money," Dallas told him.

Before Mack could speak, Dizzy spoke, "Nigga your ass just came back from the dead. Are you complaining about leaving this life? What the fuck is wrong with you? If you've got a death wish, I can kill your bitch ass now." Dizzy is pissed.

"Nigga who the fuck are you talking to like that?" Mack can't believe Dizzy.

"Yo bitch ass no one got time for this shit. The boss said it over, so it's over, null and void, now deal with it." Dizzy stand toe to toe with Mack.

"My nigga got a heart. I'm proud of you boy because you used to have a nigga like me wondering," Mack stated. The whole room laughed because they know Mack thought Dizzy was a fun kid.

Dizzy grabs him hugging him. "I missed you, nigga. I respect your hustle, but I don't want to bury you, my nigga. We got a lot to live for." Dizzy held him tight.

Mack doesn't know what reason he has to live. He often questions why God allowed him to come back this time. He is there for some reason. Mack just couldn't put his finger on it at the moment. The phone speaker broke Mack thoughts. "Dallas you have an incoming call that you must take now," the moderator told him.

"Is it private or can I just pick up?" The speaker is the new call screener that you must speak to before your call is transfer to the boss.

"It's a conference caller that asked you to put them on speaker phone," the speaker told him.

That statement made beads of sweat form on Dallas's head. He doesn't know what is going on, but he did as he asks. "Speak," he stated into the phone.

"Dallas it's great to be talking with you again love," the mystery woman told him. The voice caused Dizzy, Mack, and Zane to look at each other with crazy expressions.

"Ahhhhh what did I do to deserve this call, love?" She laughs because she knows that her voice always makes him nervous.

"It not you that made me call. It is Mack." Dallas knows that his new place is wire, and it doesn't surprise him one bit.

"Wasting no time huh boss on getting the inside scoop." Dallas let her know that he knows she is watching him.

"I have to keep my eyes on all my investments. I am a business person and a business man like you watches his investments. Nisha should know that best right?" Nisha looked at the phone.

"Who the fuck is this bitch? She doesn't know me," Nisha popped off too soon.

"I am the bitch that controls everything including the air you breathe. Be careful what you say when you talk to me. I love that gangsta that lives inside of you but so that you know; that won't help you with me because the devil lives inside of me." That statement made the room cold.

Mack broke the ice. "What's good Ms. Sexy?" He often calls her that because she is exceptional in every way.

"Why don't you want out Mack? You're not tired of this shit already? Hustling has no retirement plan baby. You walk away while it is going good," the boss told him.

"I feel that, but I don't have shit else out here to do. I am not in love like Zane or any of these other people. The streets are all I know."

Mack is pissed more so about not knowing love than leaving the life. If he had something he loved, maybe walking away would be easy. At that moment, it is the only thing he liked.

"I used to feel the same way so just keep your head up. Love will find you. I promise we will keep you busy until it does babe. At this moment, you've got a casino to bring down." She laughs Mack joins her. She never knows, but he is madly in love with her. He knows that dream will never come true due to the husband that is willing to die for her at any moment.

"Thanks, babe. When Dallas drops the ball I can always count on you to keep it rolling." Mack smiles at the phone.

"Indeed. Dallas until next time." She hangs up, leaving just as smoothly as she came.

"Indeed," Dallas mumbled. He had mad respect for that woman.

The room was quiet when Shannon asked, "So you all gonna tell us who she is because she knows our every fucking move?" Dallas, Mack, Dizzy, and Zane all looked away.

"Zane," Shannon calls him out because he is the one she is giving pussy.

"Baby I can't. Don't do me like that you will find out in due time. All I can say when it comes to the boss lady." Zane looked away from her cold stare.

"I thought you were the boss Dallas?" Jay asked.

"I am! As you know, every boss has a boss boo." The men in the room nod their heads as they agree.

"We wish you had told us that a bitch is running shit around here. Give me my fucking money so I can go home to my kids and husband." Jasmine feels some way about that shit. She is glad that after that, it will be all over, and she could go back to being a mom and a wife. Little did she know it's a little too late.

"The cashier that you passed on the way in has them." Dallas knows that they were pissed.

The women walked out; Zane calls, "Shannon baby see you at home later." He is kissing ass.

"No, you won't." She rolls her eyes going with her girls.

"Damn!" Zane knew that shit was coming. The other men shake their heads busting out laughing.

Zane sits back, lighting a blunt since there is no need to run home.

Chapter 9

Jasmine is feeling some way about the bitch that called and how she talked to Nisha. She is Dallas's Capo, not theirs. Jasmine got her check heading home. She is pissed but the moment her eyes set on that seventy-five-thousand-dollar check, she knows that the shit is worth it. Or so Jasmine believes. Money moves Jasmine in a major way, but she doesn't understand that some shit you just can't buy.

Jasmine hopped out of the whip begin to climb the forty steps that it takes to get to her third-floor apartment. She is glad that with all the money she has made and saved she will be leaving this hellhole going into a new house. Jasmine unlocks the door noticing that her house is too damn quiet for a woman with four kids and a husband.

"I'm home," she yells. The kids usually run to her asking if she brought them something back.

This time, she doesn't get the answer that she is looking for and needs at that moment. Jasmine heads to her bedroom figuring that Korey took them to the park. She needs a nap anyway, so she is going to embrace that alone time because she needed that too.

As Jasmine lay on the bed, seeing a folded letter. Jasmine opens it, and her heart begins to break as she read it.

Dear Wife,

I left you this letter so that you will not trip too much. I see that you have a new life that is important to you. I understand that it's making you lots of money. Yes, money is great, but I feel that I have too much to lose if karma decides to knock at your door someday. I have tried over and over again to get you to pick a side. When you chose the last job, over your family. I know this position hold your heart more than we do. So I got a small place for me and my kids on the Southside of town. You can visit them, but you will have to take me to court to get them back. I am sure all of that will come up in divorce court. Oh yeah, I filed the papers because of the only way I am going to bury my wife is from poor health or old age. Not because she chooses a life that got her gunned down in the streets. If you ever go to jail, you might as well be dead cause me, or my kids will not visit a place like that.

I won't hold you up. I am sure you've got a new mission to handle. Just call before you come. Goodbye, 314-444-6869.

P.S. I still love you just not enough to stay and watch you do this.

Jasmine is numb. She doesn't know how to register the information that she has taken in. She never in a million years thought he would leave her or take her kids. How could he? She begins to cry as she walks the floor. Jasmine doesn't know what to do. Jasmine wants to kill the bastard for making her hurt this way. All she is trying to do is make a better life for her family. Korey sorry ass sure isn't trying to change things. What else is she to do? Jasmine knows that she can't call or visit him right then. She is a mess. The state of mind Jasmine is in; she could have killed him.

Jasmine needs someone to talk too. She picks up the phone dialing the number.

"How can I help you?" Dizzy jokes as he answered the phone. Jasmine doesn't say anything because if she opens her mouth she will breakdown crying.

"What happened Jasmine?" Dizzy could feel her pain through the phone.

"He took them; I don't know what to do right now. I feel like I'm going to lose my mind. I didn't think he would do this to me," Jasmine cries.

"Come over. We can talk, okay." Dizzy have to help her because she helped him in his time of need.

"Ok give me your address," Jasmine said.

Dizzy gave it to her and then said, "Jasmine drive safe." Dizzy ended the call. He shakes his head because it is not the time for that shit, he couldn't blame the ole boy. If Jasmine were his wife she wouldn't be doing that shit, he knows that.

Tequila knows the date that she and Dizzy are sharing is about to come to an end. Tequila likes him a lot. She doesn't know what it is about the man that is driving her wild. When his phone rang all the other times, he ignored it, so the lady that is calling has to be important to him. Tequila is hoping that she is not so important that she got in her way because that wouldn't be good. Tequila is going to have Dizzy no matter what or who tries to get in her way. Nothing could stop her once she has love on her mind.

"I'm sorry about this. A female friend of mine is having trouble on the home front." Dizzy is straight Tequila likes that.

"I understand. I just hope she doesn't make a habit of this throughout our relationship." She smiles but the statement made him choke.

"Relationship? Baby slow down. Good things come to those that wait." Dizzy plays it off, but he thinks this heffa is crazy.

"I just want her to know that I plan to wait forever if I have too." Tequila was all over him. She is rubbing and touching his man part. He likes it, but it is not the time. The lady is starting to scare him the doorbell rang, and he is glad.

"Baby I've got to get that." Dizzy peels her hands off him.

"Go ahead, Daddy." Tequila is sexy in a strange, crazy way.

As he walked to open the door, Tequila pulls the dress she wearing over her head to reveal a sexy one piece that she has on under there. She knows that she isn't going to get the goods, but she wants to make the woman think so.

Chapter 10

Jasmine steps in once Dizzy open the door.

He hugs her giving her a peck on the cheek.

Tequila doesn't like that gesture, but she played it

cool, as she acts as if she is gathering her things to

leave his place. Dizzy turns around to see her

entire ass with a thong placed lovely in the crack.

His eyes almost popped out of his head.

"Oh damn! I'm sorry. I didn't mean to fuck

up your night D. I can dip, go have me a drink, and

fuck with you tomorrow." That's what Jasmine's

mouth said, but she feels some way about the other

woman in the room.

Dizzy is about to speak, but Tequila spoke

first. "Oh no honey come on in. I am leaving. I

know how it can be when you just need a good friend to talk. Pay me no mind at all." She smiles.

"Baby I think that it would be easier to pay you no mind if you put your clothing on." His dick is hard, and Jasmine sees it growing.

She laughed, pulled the dress back over her head, and placed her shoes on her feet. She walked over to Dizzy and said, "Until next time daddy." She kisses him with so much passion he wants to kick Jasmine's ass out and fuck the bitch's brains out, but family came first.

"Indeed indeed." He watched that ass float pass him. The boy almost wants to cry.

Jasmine watched him lust after the bitch, and she doesn't like it. However, she pushed the shit out of her mind because she has too much going on right then to be in her feelings about some shit that has nothing to do with her. Dizzy isn't her man, so she doesn't know why she is jealous, but she is.

Nisha knows that Jay is acting funny when she dropped her off, but she let the shit go because she is still tight about the bitch that called talking that boss shit. That shit rubbed her the wrong fucking way. She is glad it is the last mission now that she knows there is some strange bitch behind the scenes running shit. Now that Dallas has pulled that crap, he better hope that she makes it to the next mission. At that point, she has enough money to leave town and never look back. If he wants her, he would have to come looking for her.

Nisha has some thinking to do, and she knows that she doesn't have much time to do it. Nisha knows that she better makes her next move her best move. If she doesn't it is going to cost her life.

Jay is being followed she is sick of this shit it is time to face the issue. Jay is meeting up with Q in a minute. She wants to be with him today because she doesn't know if she will ever see him again after tonight. Jay plans to deal with her demons and face whatever fate has in store for her. One thing she knows for sure is that she can't go on living like that for the more fucking day.

Jay entered the house to find Q sitting on the couch.

"Babe I am glad you home because I need to holla at you about something," he stated as he looks over at her.

"What's good boo?" Jay flopped down on the couch next to him. It felt good to take a load off.

"I know that we haven't been together long, but no other woman has ever made me feel like you. I want this feeling for the rest of my life. I guess what I am trying to say is, will you marry me?" Q is smiling from ear to ear. He is glad that he finally got it off his chest. Moving on to the next step in life, he reached into his pocket to get the ring box out. As he is about to open it, Jay stopped him. She doesn't want to see a ring.

"Q I love you, but I can't marry you, babe." She hates the words the moment they left her mouth, but what other choice does she have.

"What!" Q couldn't believe the phrase that has just left the woman that stole his heart's mouth. That is not how he envisioned things going. He is looking for jumping up and down, kisses, hugs, screams, and tears. He got I can't marry you. Where they do that at?

"Q don't be angry, please. I love you like I said, but there are so many levels of my life that you don't know. If you did you wouldn't be able to handle it." Jay is now on her feet. She isn't in the mood for that. She just wanted to come home, chill, and hopefully get her pussy ate and smoke a blunt before heading out to confront her stalker. But no, this nigga just had to come up with some bullshit like this. Just like a nigga, always offering shit that you never want.

"Don't be angry? I bought this fucking ring, cut off every bitch I used to fuck with for yo ass, and you have the nerve to holler don't be angry! Shit Jay? I can't believe that I am this fucking stupid." Q shakes his head as he jumps off the couch stuffing each foot inside his shoes because he knows it is time to get the fuck up out of there fast.

"Where are you going? I never meant to hurt you! I do love you boo. It's just that I don't have a regular job love and marriage is not the right thing right now," Jay told him.

"Your friend Jasmine is married and her sister Shannon is dating about to marry that nigga Zane. So marriage just doesn't work for you, not your job, because they cooperate with you too.

"That's not fair, and you know it. Jasmine is about to lose her damn husband, and Shannon's man is a part of the life we live. That's how they met, so it's different. They both know what they stand to lose. They're cool with that. Whereas you don't know what you stand to lose, and I can't choose between you and this right now." Jay is honest.

"I never asked you to choose if your life is that damn dangerous, why did you fuck with my heart and my head? You should have told me that you were not looking for love or a lifelong thing, and I would have known how to play my hand." Q is stuffing all the things he has in the apartment in a bag.

"I do want those things someday!" Jay doesn't know what else to say. She is losing the man she has grown to love when she needs him the most. She shakes her head.

Q carried two duffle bags on his back, and he looks at her with a tear stained face. "Today is just not that day huh?" Jay is heartbroken. She never meant for shit to get that bad, but it had and fast. One-minute Jay getting money and loving life, the next has a man that wants to wife her and one that stalking her. Jay needs to handle this shit to do that she knows that she has to let Q go.

"No it's not, and I'm sorry." Jay flopped back down on her couch. She wants to cry, but there is no need. Jay brought all that shit on herself. All she could think is karma a bitch that has come to fuck her.

"I'm sorry too. Goodbye, Jay." Q know that he would never love or look at women the same once he got over his heartache. Men don't like as fast and when they do the pain of rejection or mistreatment is a hundred times worse than what a woman feels when she is betrayed. That's why if you ever meet a man and his heart seems to be cold, you can thank the bitch before you. She damaged his soul.

Jay watched him walk out of her life. There is nothing that she could do right then, but hopefully, when she handled the stalker and did the last mission, she could try to get him back. Only time would tell. She had too much shit going on to bow down. She smoked her blunt, picked up the phone, and called Jasmine.

Chapter 11

Zane is watching Shannon sleep; she looks peaceful. Shannon has been in the bed ever since she got home from the meeting earlier. It shocks him how much he loves his family life. Jailah came into the bedroom where Zane and her mom are. "Zane," she calls him.

"Yes, Ms. Ja." He has given her that nickname.

"Somebody's at the door." She is four going on forty-four.

Zane laughed. "Thanks, babe." He doesn't know who could be at Shannon's door.

He opens the door to see an Ice Cube looking ass nigga. "Can I help you, playboy?" Zane asked.

"I'm looking for my baby mama nigga," the chubby guy informed him.

Zane chuckles because he'd heard of the clown. "Oh, so you John Huh?" he asked.

"Yeah that's me," the nigga boasted.

"Well my wife is sleeping. She is with child so I'd rather not wake her unless it's important," Zane told him.

"Wife? With child? Nigga, please! You have to be out your rabbit ass mind." John is pissed.

"My nigga, you seem upset about something." Zane know what he is doing rubbing shit in his face.

"Never that! I am over that bitch, my nigga. You can have her. That pussy is tired and used up anyway," John bragged not understanding who the fuck he is talking to.

Zane steps back like he is about to walk away from the door, then turned around and knocked John the hell out. The shit happened so fast John doesn't know what hit him.

Jailah is standing there watching, and she ran to wake her mother. "Mommy! Mommy! Zane's in trouble," she said. Hitting always got her in trouble.

Shannon looked at her and asked, "What he do Jailah?" She is still half-asleep.

"He hit my daddy," she stated like it is nothing.

"What? You have to be kidding me." Shannon jumped out of the bed and ran to the living room.

"What have you done Zane?" Shannon asked.

"This ain't my fucking fault. This hoe ass nigga was talking shit, and I laid his bitch ass down," Zane stated as he held John's ankle and Mack held him by the wrist.

"Why the hell did you call Mack's crazy ass over here?" Shannon asked.

Before Zane could speak, Mack told her, "He didn't call me. I came over here to visit your ugly ass."

Jaliah laughed, "He called you ugly and Mack cussing." She is amused by the whole ordeal.

Zane finally realized that she is in the room. He drops John's legs that caused Mack to release the nigga as well. "I'm sorry love. I didn't mean to hit your daddy. Uncle Mack is sorry for cursing."

"Yeah cutie pie I am," Mack assured her.

"It's ok! Is my dad dead?" Jailah asked.

"He's about to be!" Mack forgot he was talking to a child. Zane nudges him thinking the nigga had to be crazy. John begins to groan from his injuries. Zane looked at Jaliah and said, "No he's not boo." He hugs her. "I'm sorry about this." He wants her to know that he doesn't mean to hurt her.

"It's okay, but Mommy's gonna whoop you when everyone leaves because hitting is not nice," she warned him.

Zane laughed. "I will be looking forward to taking my spanking." Shannon shakes her head and he winked at her.

"Jailah please escort your mother back into the bedroom for me?" Zane asked her.

"Ok, I will. Mommy let's go so the boys can chat." Mack finds her to the cutest little girl ever.

As Shannon is exiting the room, John is pulling his fat ass off the ground. "Nigga I'm gonna kill your bitch ass," he threatened Zane.

"Or you could get your huge ass up and out of here before I let my man take you outside and do you dirty," Zane gave him a choice.

John thought about the offer. He knows that he is outnumbered. His best bet is to walk away. He started to say something on his way out of the apartment. The look in Mack's eyes told him that the man holding the gun is no stranger to death. John exited the apartment building thinking to himself that it is not over.

Mack shakes his head at the situation. Shannon walks back in the living room to see Mack and Zane laughing about how that nigga John was laid out like a whore.

"What's funny?" She knows that she needs to link up with her girls.

"Yo ass for dating that clown ass nigga," Mack told her.

"Yeah, that's right, because you pick them so well?" Shannon is bitchy.

"Babe stop acting like that boobie." Zane walked over to Shannon and kissed her. He knows this pregnancy is going to be hard for him, but at the end, he would be the happiest man alive.

"Man don't be kissing her ass. She is spoiled enough already." Mack is going to drive Shannon crazy while she carried his little niece or nephew.

"Mack yo ass gonna get out of my house if you are going to keeps talking shit." Shannon wanted to slap his punk ass.

"Girl I ain't going nowhere so get your ass on somewhere with your mean ugly ass." Zane know that his homey is enjoying himself as he is driving his wife insane.

"Nigga that's enough already," Zane fussed at Mack knowing that he enjoying himself

"Naw its real baby I got his Lemonheads ass, but right now, I need you to keep an eye on

Jailah for me. I need to step out with my girls." Shannon knew that it is time to link up so they could rap.

"No worries boo. Go ahead and do you. Ms. Ja and I will be all right." He felt she needed that girl time with her friends. It had been awhile.

"Thanks, boo," Shannon said and kissed him.

"Your ass calls me Lemonheads again, and it's gonna be something," Mack stated as he rolled a blunt.

"Whatever nigga." Shannon exited the room so she could get her night started.

Shannon had got in touch with Jay who told her that Jasmine is at Dizzy's house. She isn't going to meet up with them because she has some shit on her mind as well. Jay is down she plans to face her stalker after she met with the girls. Nisha is game too she needed to get out, but she wasn't planning to share the thoughts on her mind. The shit she was thinking could cause her to get killed. They all agreed to meet at 54th Street Bar & Grill.

Chapter 12

The statuesque woman stood in the huge window that went from the floor to the ceiling. She never would've imagined living like that. As she thought back over her life thinking about where she had come from. She grew up with nothing and struggled to make something of her life. Now she lived in a three point five million dollars' home and drove a limited addition Aston Martin. She never really wanted that much, and still, here she was.

Medallion walked in the room behind her and wrapped his arms around her slim waist pressing his manhood against her supple ass. He was deep chocolate, hard body, standing five foot ten. He was an athletic man with salt and pepper dreads and a matching goatee. He was a good-looking man for his age. Often he was beating the younger women off with a stick for two reasons. One, they had nothing on his wife, and second, his wife had always been known as a deadly weapon. He wasn't ready to die.

"Babe what are you doing gazing out this big ass window? Come back to bed. We miss you." She knew who he was speaking of when he said we.

The woman laughed, "You're so nasty." She loved the love that man had burning in him all these years. The love just never seemed to get old.

"You married me cause I'm nasty so why you complaining now?" Medallion licked and nibbled at her.

"I didn't marry you for that reason," she giggled.

"Well tell me why you married me," he said and kissed her again.

"Because you were a G." She remembered how he represented that thug life with class. Some people thought that hustlers were unorthodox. Which was far from true. Really, hustlers knew there were key essentials to the game. Medallion followed the essentials of the game to the letter that's why they standing strong today.

"Oh is that right?" He continued to kiss her neck.

"Yes baby." She turned to face him.

"Why are we going backwards?" She had been wanting to ask. She thought they were out of the game for good. Then she came to find out that Dallas was signing off. It was his last mission. He would still hustle and have working girls, but no more big licks for him. She was worried about where that would leave Mack. She knew Zane could live with the decision whereas Mack lived for that life.

"We're going back because you're a hustler's mother," Medallion schooled her. He always kept it real with her because she was smart and could see though all his lies.

"Yes I am and I wear that title which a badge of honor." She knew that it was a life that you choose to get into, but had to die to get out of.

She knew that with her son taking over the drug game that her family had built she was going to need to be close by. The game had changed and the cowards outweighed the real gangsters that were left out there. She was grateful that Dallas had kept her in the game that long, but she'd had enough now that she was about to be thirty-five and her only born son was going to turn twenty-one the same day. It was now time to pass the torch.

Deep down inside the lady wished that her whole family could just walk away but it wasn't like that. People tell you can get out but the truth is that you're in that shit for life.

Medallion was still kissing her when the house phone rang. He eyed the number as it popped across the screen.

"Get the phone babe," she told him.

"I don't want to." He knew that he wasn't about to get any pussy tonight.

"Don't do that. I won't stay on long and I will suck your dick as soon as I get off," she promised knowing what her man needed.

"Bet." He picked up the phone.

"Do you ever sleep?" Medallion asked.

"Not when I feel my sister's heart is aching," the female caller told him.

"Her pussy hurts when she's with me." Medallion was something else to be an old man.

"Boy bye! Get my sister please," the woman ordered him.

Medallion gave his love the phone and she smiled. "Hey baby cakes! How's the world treating you because it's been hard on my mind?" She was glad that she had her best friend and blood sister all rolled up in one person.

"It all good with me but you know I always feel your pain," she stated thinking about the time her hand had the most horrible burning sensation yet she hadn't burned herself. Whereas her sister had a permanent burn on her hand from wasting hot grease on it when she was cooking one evening.

"I'm sorry sis. I don't mean to fuck with your mind. It's just knowing that Dallas is ending it all as I told him he could and my boy taking over has my heart in limbo. I never thought this day would come so soon. Yet here I am facing the life I chose for my family. Why couldn't I have just been normal, went to college, became a lawyer, or some other shit." She was stressing bad. Medallion hated it. He wasn't even in the mood to get his dick sucked anymore, he just wanted to hold her and tell that things would be fine.

"It's ok. We never had a normal life if you think back on it. Some people are just built to do different thing sis and this was our thing. One way in and no way out." She tried to comfort her sister.

"Yup this is our fucked up life, but I am gonna deal with it like the G I was born to be." She had to pull all that shit together and woman up. Yes, her only child was about to take over the family business and at any time could be pulled in to a war zone, but it was what it was. He had been groomed all his life for that so there was no turning back now. Life deals the cards; we have to play the game. She just wanted to be around to teach him when to hold them and when to fold them.

"Well I can't stay up all night. I just wanted to make peace with this and there is only one way to do that," her sister told her.

"How so sis?" She didn't think she wanted to know the answer.

"I'm coming back with you. We started together and we will finish together," she assured her.

"I love you Vicious," Venom told her.

"Not more that I love you Venom. You started the Duffle Bag crew. Now that Mellow Jr. about to take over it's gonna be hard on us cause we both know the game can be very cold. So we're gonna be in the background to make sure that he doesn't freeze up.

"I'm with that. Is Black cool with this?" Venom asked.

"I haven't told him yet. Don't worry. Goodnight sis." Vicious ended the call.

Chapter 13

Dallas knows that the time for shit to end would come. He didn't know that when it came, he would be alone. He just never allowed anyone in because he doesn't want to break the heart of a woman that he claims he loves. It is hard to say you love someone when you're dedicated to something bigger than your whole life, and one false move could end your life.

Dallas opted to stay single. He feels that it is the best thing to do. Now he isn't so sure that he made the right choice. What would he do now? Dallas doesn't have anyone to share the money with, and Dallas isn't sure if he could trust that the love is for real, or if it is the money, they are after.

Dallas is not a soft nigga by far, but after you watch life taken from a human body, you often wonder why you're still there. Wondering why God saw fit to keep you around all this time. He doesn't know the reasoning behind it all. Dallas is just going to have to keep living to he figures it all out.

He looked over at his potnas and smiling that Zane has it all together with his lil family and shit. Zane had dropped his lil stepdaughter off to her grandmother's house because his wife and the Duffle Bag Ladies are having an outing.

Yes, they have earned the title of Ladies. They handled everything with class. Well almost all of them. That damn Nisha acts as if she just couldn't get it together. There is something up with her Dallas can't put his finger on, that bothers him. Now isn't the time to dwell on it, plus what's done in the dark always comes to the light.

"Man why you over there all googly-eyed and shit? You're the one that decided to shut down shop." Mack is still pissed about that.

"Shut your coma toasted ass up nigga. You should be glad you're breathing," Dallas told him joking.

"No thanks to you my nigga." Mack couldn't believe that he had just said that. There is some underlying hurt from being left for dead, and he feels that Dallas is about to leave him hanging again.

"Really? That's how you feel huh?" The truth hurt Dallas. Zane just shakes his head. He hates to see his family fall apart like that. Mack is out of line because he knows the consequences that came with the lifestyle. It is screwed up for him to play the game raw like that.

"My bad cuz, I'm fucked up behind this shutting down shop shit. That's not how I feel. I know what I was getting into when I signed up for this mess. That why I'm tripping. Now that we're getting out, I don't know what I'm supposed to do with life. This nigga Zane promised that we would travel the world. Now he's got a family and shit, so that's out. I apologize from my heart for that slick shit I just said." Mack is a good dude, and he is afraid of change.

"Don't worry about that shit nigga, but that's one of the reasons I'm glad we're hanging up the towel. I can't stomach burying one of you niggas. You niggas the only family I have ever had for real," Dallas admitted.

"We're still your fucking family," Zane assured him.

Dallas chuckled. "Check this nigga out, got a wife, baby on the way and shit." Dallas is happy for him.

"I know right, Shannon came in, put that pussy on that nigga, and the boy got stupid didn't he," Mack cosigned what Dallas said.

"Fuck the pussy! That bitch had him sucked at the moment she stepped in this bitch," Dallas teased remembering that day that Zane first laid eyes on her.

"True dat," Mack said dying laughing. Zane doesn't find shit funny.

"Aye, you two can kill that noise for real." Zane doesn't like the way they just took his player's card from him.

"Niggas chill the hell out. You're walking away from this shit a winner, unlike our lonely asses." Mack laughed because he had just admitted that he feels alone.

Mack's phone began to ring. "Hello?" He doesn't know the number.

"Hey, babe can I come over tonight?" Tasha asked.

"I'm not home. I'm out chilling with my potnas." He is hoping that she would just let the shit be, yet he knows that she isn't going to give up that easy.

"No worries. I will be up late, just call me please." She is sexy and begging, how could he say no.

"Alright, girl I will call you later." Mack hangs up shaking his head.

"Let us guess who that is," Zane teased. He looked at Dallas, and the two acted as if they are thinking hard.

"Tasha," both busting out laughing.

Mack doesn't think that shit is funny. That girl has been on him since high school. He didn't fuck her until they were grown up and that shit caused her to become worse than what she was. "How do you know?" he asked.

"The crazy heffa keeps calling here asking for you even after we told her you were dead," Dizzy stated.

Everyone looked at him because no one heard him come in. Now that fool joined the conversation like he'd been there for hours.

"Well look what the wind blew in," Dallas said.

"Happy to see you all too." Dizzy is sarcastic

as he shakes his head. Zane could tell that something is bothering him "What's the matter bloodbath?" he asked.

"Man, I just had to do the hardest shit I've ever done in my life." Dizzy is still shaking his head.

"Do tell my nigga." Dallas is a nosey muthafucka, but that's what keeps him in the game because he always had a heads up on the next person.

"Man looks, Jasmine came to my place." Mack cut him off, "You let her in the dungeon?" He is shocked because it had taken years for that nigga to allow them in.

"Man, no. I moved," Dizzy stated. Mack doesn't know what the hell is going on. Dizzy had a new place, Zane getting married and having a baby, and it is the last mission. He is overwhelmed by it all.

Dizzy continued, "Man she called me crying because her husband left a letter stating that he moved out and took the kids. So I told her to come over to talk," he said to them. The fellas can't believe that the nigga left her.

"Now mind I had a bad little bitch there. Tequila is the property manager for the compound. I told her I am gonna take a rain check on our little gathering." The men feel him because Jasmine is family so that bitch is going to have to wait.

"She was hurt not meaning to mess up your date," Dallas assured him.

"Fuck the date! She came over, and the bitch left. Jasmine got to talking; she cried, and I comforted her until she is back smiling and laughing. Then we started kissing I picked her up and sat her on my lap. I am sucking her titties and squeezing her ass." Dizzy had to stop talking for a minute cause thinking about it made his dick hard.

"My Nii GGG GA!" Mack patted him on the back. Zane and Dallas are laughing.

"Y'all are not going to believe what I did. I am playing with the pussy, and it is gushing, sticky, warm, and wet. Just as I am about to taste it; I stopped. She is like, 'What's the matter?' I am like we can't do this." He shakes his head. "Jasmine is like, but I want to, I told her no you don't. You hurt behind what your husband has done." After that, she got a call from the girls I had to leave." He sits quietly in deep thought.

"Are you fucking serious?" Mack yells.

"You have to be out your fucking mind," Zane stated.

"Nigga you had the pussy in your hands and you gave it back?" Dallas ask because he just doesn't understand.

Dizzy know that he is going to catch hell about the decision he made. He wants to be with her so badly, but he doesn't want it to in a vulnerable state. He wants to make sure that it is what she wants to do. "I know you niggas are gonna clown me because I didn't take it. I wanted that bitch bad, but the timing is off." Jasmine has his head fucked up. He started back talking, "The funniest shit though is that her pussy smelled sweet like vanilla, and I could tell that it is a natural smell," he said with a smile.

Zane smiled because he knows what Dizzy is speaking on. "That must run in the family. Be careful cause once you taste it pussy will never taste the same again." Zane knows that's why he had to have Shannon for life.

"I don't want to touch no bitch with magic vanilla extract pussy," Mack said.

"Me either, I am good; you niggas can have that shit," Dallas said, and they all busted out laughing. Zane was sure that Dizzy's soul wouldn't be able to rest until Jasmine was his.

Chapter 14

The girls Nisha, Shannon, and Jay, had met up, and Jasmine is running late since she changed her mind on joining them. They are having drinks, talking, and bobbing to the music. It feels good to be together. It has been awhile since everything has taken place.

Shannon is drinking soda, yet she still was having a great time. She loves her liquor but loves her unborn child and man more. Nisha isn't used to that Shannon, and she doesn't like it. The truth is Nisha is jealous that Shannon has found a good catch, unlike their brother.

"Um, I see Zane got shit in check. Look at this bitch over here drinking soda," Nisha throws shade.

"You damn right he does! Who mad? You!" Shannon chopped her ass down. Jay knows that Nisha is starting shit for no reason at all.

"Never mad. Please! I just couldn't have no nigga running me; that's all I'm saying." Nisha is pissed.

"Yeah ok, my brother used to run that ass and your money. He just doesn't fuck with you anymore." Shannon sipped her soda thinking about how she never really cared for Nisha. She is glad that her brother had left that ass for real.

"Get it right boo. I don't fuck with Staccz, okay," Nisha tried to play it like she ended the relationship. Jay and Shannon know that is a lie.

"Damn we fighting already?" Jasmine asked coming up to the table.

"Girl no. Shannon is popping shit because she thinks Zane is the cream of the crop." Nisha is in her box.

Jay and Shannon looked at Nisha as if she is crazy. She is the one who started all this. "See that right there is why my brother doesn't fuck with you. You lie so much. It's unbelievable how you do that," Shannon stated.

"And from the looks of the ten karat ring Shannon rocking he's most definitely the cream of the crop," Jay added.

The three all started laughing. Nisha doesn't find shit funny and neither would Shannon once she showed Zane that lovely pussy of hers. "So what are we meeting for anyway? I got things to do." Nisha said.

"We're glad to see you too Nisha. Anyways I'm here because me and Q broke up," Jay said with sadness in her eyes.

"That's why you're helping Shannon dick ride Zane," Nisha says.

"Not actually. We broke up because Q proposed to me and I said no," Jay informed her hating ass.

"Why Jay?" Shannon and Jasmine asked. Nisha is just pissed because everybody is in love but her.

"I have demons to face and other obligations to deal with, so the timing is off. Q just doesn't understand the lifestyle we live. Q would make this job harder than it already is. I love him, so I have to let him go for now. If it's meant to be, it will come back to me. He has a ring and everything," Jay sighed hoping that it isn't the end.

"You're right Jay. The job we do makes it hard to marry or be married. When I got home today, Korey and the kids were gone." Jasmine

wants to cry all over again.

"Girl get the fuck out of here!" Shannon

can't believe that bull crap. He must have lost his

mind running off with the kids. Shannon doesn't

pop off like she wanted to. She was going to hear

her sister out.

"Yes. Korey left me a letter and everything

telling me where they are and a number to reach

them. Talking about he still loves me but he can no

longer support me in this." Jasmine begins to cry.

Jay hugs her as Shannon held her hand and

rubbed it. Nisha is looking at her thinking that's

what her dumb ass gets. She had a great husband

yet she out there trying to be a gangsta. "Well I don't feel bad for you," Nisha said.

Jasmine's eyes blazed with fire. "You bitch! I am about to kill you." Nisha jumps back as Jasmine reached for her. Jay grabbed Jasmine because she knows that she is dealing with a lot of stress. Nisha is in bitch mode for no reason.

"Nisha that shit ain't cool," Shannon told her. She is ready to slap the hell out of Nisha.

"I don't give a flying fuck. After this mission, all this shit will be over, and I will be done dealing with all of you. Because you all never liked me anyway! You just tolerated me because of my children. It's all good; I have real friends."

Nisha storms out pissed. No one understood why when she is the main one popping off at the mouth.

"Fuck that bitch! She's right; I never liked her dirty ass. She is going to have the nerve to say she doesn't feel sorry for me. Ain't that's a lousy bitch ass hoe?" Jasmine is going in. She was livid.

The people in the restaurant were looking at the commotion. It was normal to see people wild out like that in the STL. The land of "I don't give a fuck where we at, if you are tripping you can get it." That's just how it went down there. The waitress came over. "Is everyone okay?" she asked.

"Bitch do we looking like something is wrong?" Jasmine barked.

The waitress is speechless. She doesn't know what to do next, so she said, "Not at all can I take your order?" She is sweating and flushed in the face.

"Give us some damn hot wings," Jasmine said still in rare form.

The waiter scribbled on the pad and hustled away. The waitress doesn't give a fuck about the wings. She just wants to be as far away from the craziest lady she'd ever met in her life. Shannon and Jay are bugging up at her scary ass. Shannon jumped in and said, "You all want to hear something hilarious?" Jay and Jasmine needs a laugh.

"Yeah," they both chimed.

"Zane knocked John the fuck out today to make it even funnier. Jailah asked Zane is John dead." Shannon is crying laughing.

Jay damn near spit her drink all over everyone. "Get the fuck out of here," Jay managed to say.

Shannon gave them the rundown on what took place. Insight on why she wanted to get out and chill with the girls it is much needed. Something is up with Nisha. Shannon can't put her finger on what it is at the moment.

"Guess what?" Jasmine asked after Shannon finished telling her story.

"What?" asked Shannon.

"I almost slept with Dizzy," Jasmine confessed.

"Bullshit!" Shannon can't believe it.

"Yes, I went over there after I got the letter from Korey. Don't ask me why I called him instead of one of you guys. We were talking, and I was crying. He held me, and I kissed him. One thing led to another." Jasmine shakes her head.

"You said almost. What stopped it cause that man is good-looking?" Jay needed to know why it didn't go down.

"Dizzy ended it saying he doesn't want it to happen like that. He wanted me to be sure that it is what I want to do." Jasmine shakes her head again because, at that moment, she does want to, but with her situation and timing, she is glad that he is the man that he is.

"OMG," is all that Shannon could say.

"Well today has been a helluva day," Jasmine said throwing her drink back.

"I will drink to that," Jay tossed her drink back as well. They all enjoyed a laugh along with the rest of their evening.

Chapter 15

Mack bopped his head to the music as he scopes out the room. Zane had run off to drain the central vein. Nigga had too many Bud Ices. The honey's up in the place are banging tonight from the hair to the shoes. Mack loves the life he lives. It isn't as fulfilling as it used to be. There is no gratification in the shit anymore. You never know when you are going to be robbed, locked up, or killed.

Top shit off, you don't even know which woman you can trust. Hell, Mack worked with four of the sexiest bitches' men had ever seen. They used sex appeal to get close to what a nigga is holding. He shakes his head thinking about his life and how it has turned out. Mack dodged a trip to heaven once, but he hopes that when he gets there, it is a helluva lot better than what he'd been dealing with down there.

"My nigga I thought we were having a great time. Why you so blue?" Zane teased Mack. He could tell the nigga has a lot on his mind.

"It's nothing man." Mack wants to enjoy his night. That is why he doesn't drink much. It caused him to be emotional.

"Come on now. Mack, it's me you're talking to," Zane said.

"Bruh looks at all the shit we've been through, and now that it's all about to end what is the real reward," Mack stated.

Zane could feel his pain cause if he didn't have Shannon. Zane wouldn't know which way to go now that it is time to call it quits. "I feel you, man. We're gonna have a nice piece of change but what are you to do with it if all you know is hood shit?" Mack has Zane thinking about what he has to offer his family. Money is no good. Shannon has her money. What would he provide his children?

"See what I'm saying, man? Hell, at least you got Shannon." Mack sipped his Hennessy.

"Yeah but what do I have to offer her and the babies? She's got her money, so what does she need me for?" Zane asked him. His mind is now fucked up.

"What the hell do you mean what do you have to offer, you a man? You've got everything that woman wants and needs," Mack assured him. He is proud of his boy for allowing love in his heart.

"What is that?" Zane is unsure of himself.

"Love nigga! It's the most valuable thing you can give to a woman. The great thing about it is that you're willing to give the love," Mack told him.

"Thanks, man. You've got love to give as well." Zane appreciated his potna.

"Yeah it's there, but I'm afraid to use it because I have never loved. I don't know what love has to offer," Mack admitted.

Zane out was done. He doesn't know what to say. His boy has never been this honest in his life with his feelings. "You should be aware love because I love you." Zane knows he needs to hear that.

Mack is waving the waiter over for another drink that he doesn't need. He is checking out the scene and spots Nisha dancing on a table. "Aye bruh, check that shit out," Mack told Zane.

"What the fuck is she doing here or up there for that matter?" Zane is confused because he knows she supposed to be with the girls.

"I'm going to get her down!" Mack hates hoe shit like this. He wonders if she knows how cheap and desperate she looks right now.

Before Zane could protest, Mack is barging through the crowd of people. Nisha is doing her thang. If you didn't know any better, you would think she was a stripper by night. Zane watched as Mack snatched Nisha off the table and dragged her back to the area where his drink is.

"Let me go," Nisha yelled.

"Bitch are you crazy?" Mack yelled.

"Nigga I am not crazy! You must be crazy grabbing me like you're my father or something."

Nisha is embarrassed because people were watching.

"You do know who you work for don't you." Mack tries to school her. Dallas didn't even allow his whores that worked the strip to act like that.

"I don't work for nobody but me. I work with Dallas in my free time, and I do as I please," Nisha informed him.

"This bitch is about to make me snap Zane. I'm up out of here." Mack made his way to the exit.

Zane watched his boy fade into the crowd. He couldn't believe how his night had turned out. Zane looked over at Nisha who is smiling from ear to ear. "Why aren't you with the girls?" he asked her.

"They're boring, I'd much rather be here with you," she told him.

"With me? You ain't here with me." Zane is sure she had too much to drink.

"Zane let's cut the bullshit. We're both grown so let's not play games." Nisha pressed her breasts up against him.

"What bullshit girl? You know Shannon's my woman," Zane reminds her.

"One night with me and I will change that." Nisha licked her lips.

Zane busted out laughing. He thought that bitch must have bumped her head or something when she got out of bed that morning. Shannon would fuck her up, and she knows it. Nisha must have a death wish. Zane sure as hell doesn't have one with her. Plus, she is nowhere near the type of woman that he would even look at twice.

Nisha is pissed off by his laughter. She doesn't find a damn thing funny. That nigga is laughing like she is a comedian telling stand up jokes. Shannon isn't all that. Why is that nigga trying to act like she is?

"What the hell is so funny?" she asked in her feelings.

"Yo ass." Zane laughed some more.

"This is not a game. I am offering you the time of your life." Nisha knows that if he fucked her Shannon would be erased from his mind.

"Every time I make love I have the time of my life, before and after this one boo. So, my dear, there is nothing you can do for me." Zane can't believe that shit. He drank the rest of his drink.

"You ain't married yet." Nisha hates rejection.

"Fucking with you won't help me get there any faster," Zane informed her as he is walking away.

Nisha stands there with a pissed look on her face and smoke coming out of her ears. Zane would pay for trying to play her like she is crazy.

The nigga would wish he had given her the dick

when she asked for it.

Chapter 16

The girls finally left the club heading home. Jasmine can't go back. She can't sleep in that house alone. Jasmine needs to be held. She doesn't know why Dizzy is her go-to guy. Maybe because she is the one he trusted in his time of need. It was well past three in the morning when his phone rang. Jasmine was about to hang up when she heard.

"H-h-Hello," in a sexy baritone sleeping voice.

"I'm sorry I woke you Dizzy," Jasmine apologized for calling so late.

"Jazz what's the matter, baby?" Dizzy asked now fully awake.

"Nothing. I'm fine leaving the Bar and Grill with the girls," she said a little tipsy.

"Oh did you make it home safely?" Dizzy asked knowing that she has been drinking.

"I can't go there," Jasmine told him.

"Come to me." Dizzy understands what it is like to feel alone and misunderstood. His deceased wife would often fuss at him about the time he put into his job knowing that it is the task that allowed her to be a stay at home mom. He never understood a woman who got mad when their husband worked a lot. Hell, some niggas don't even have a job. He also understands Korey's standpoint as well. Their line of work wouldn't be for women if you asked him. No job that you risked your life for is for women in his mind.

After he had told her that, Jasmine hung up. She parked in the parking lot of his condo. Jasmine got out, walked to the apartment, and knocked on the door. Dizzy opened the door. He is wearing Polo pajama pants and no shirt. Beautiful wavy hair laid on his chest trailing down his stomach to a happy place.

"Come on girl, you letting my air out," Dizzy told Jasmine as she stands there staring at him.

"I know I'm getting on your nerves breaking your sleep and shit." Jasmine hates to be a burden on him or anyone else for that matter.

"Look boo; you're no burden to me. You were there for me when I needed someone to believe in me the most. I can never repay you for that," Dizzy assured her that she is not bothering him.

"Thanks," was all she could say.

Dizzy smiles. "We have a meeting tomorrow night, so I think we should try to get some sleep." He is tired as hell.

"Ok, I'll sleep on the couch." Jasmine is worn out as well.

"No, you won't." Dizzy grabs her by the hand led her to the bedroom.

Jay knows that no matter the time, she is being followed, and she is sick of the shit already. As she drives, Jay sees the car tailing her. She pulled onto a side street so he could follow her. Jay knows it would be hard to kill him on the main road.

Jay decided to have a small talk with God. "Lord, I know that I don't live life as the good book says I should. Yes, I have taken a walk on the dark side. I don't think there is a point of return. I just wanted to thank you for the time I have had here. Something has got to give. I can't live with a human shadow. So Lord if now is my time just know I love and respect you. I never meant to hurt you I just did what I had to do to survive."

Jay exited the car, as if she, is checking for a flat tire. Jay doesn't see the car but suddenly heard footsteps that are eager to get to her. Jay rose to her feet and spun around. She finally stands face to face with none other than Cash.

"Why you got your gun drawn on me?" he asked. Cash is now meeting the woman that cleaned him out and stolen his heart.

"I came here to die, but I'm not going down without a fight," Jay assured him.

Cash doesn't want to kill her even though he should. He just really wanted to know why. "I ain't trying to harm you. I just want to know why you did what you did?" Cash is sincere with what he is asking.

"It is my job." Jay is honest.

"So all of it is your job?" Cash asked as if he can't believe that.

"Yes," she answered still holding the gun on him.

"You never loved me?" Cash asked her.

"No." Jay knows that is fucked up, but it was what it is.

Cash doesn't understand Saint Louis woman. He wonders how they could be so cold. The ice he got from Jay made him think of Venom.

He walked away from Jay back to his car, got in, and drove off. Jay hopped into her car placing her gun on the seat. She begins to cry thinking that itis all behind her now and that God has spared her life yet again. The tears clouded her view and mind.

Boom! Glass flew everywhere and Jay ducked as soon as she heard the sound. It doesn't keep her from being hit in the shoulder. Jay knows it is a forty-five-millimeter bullet that pierced her.

Cash doubled back and got the drop on Jay. That bitch thinks she is just going to fuck him over as if it isn't shit. She had to be out of her damn. Jay is going to die for all the money, love, and respect Cash lost. He walked up to the car sees her hunched over, but isn't sure if she was dead.

Mack is heading home from the club. When he turned onto his street, he sees Jay's car and wondered what the hell she is doing at his place at this time of night. He noticed that something is off when he sees a nigga that looked familiar to him.

Tasha asked, "What's the matter?" She noticed his mood had changed. She loves this man with her whole soul. The small things that others would never pick up on she did.

Mack had forgotten that quick that he picked her up. It is the wrong fucking time for her to be in the car. It is what it is, though, and he is about to find out how much she loved him. As he watched dude open Jay's car door, Mack started talking fast.

"Look, Tasha, I ain't got time to explain shit right now but this what I need you to do. Drive around the block, park, and call the police. Tell them you heard shooting on the next block and you're afraid for your life. Then come back to get me, baby," Mack said as he exited the car.

Tasha asked no questions and reversed the car backward doing just as he asked. Mack crept around to the passenger side of Jay's car. The closer he got the easier he could hear what dude was saying to her, yet Jay isn't moving.

"Bitch you came all the way to South Carolina to fuck my life up, and you don't even give a shit." Cash is crying.

Mack can't believe that nigga has tracked her down after a year or more, and the nigga is heartbroken behind that shit. Mack beginning to hate his lifestyle by the minute. He knows he isn't

getting out today.

Jay moaned in pain. She hit on the side also.

Mack saw that she needed his help badly. Cash

bent over to pull Jay from the car. "Bitch you're

gonna pay for all you took from me." Cash reached

for her, and Jay is trying to reach for her gun but

the pain running through her body is damn nearly

unbearable.

Mack has the nigga right where he wants

him. He spotted Tasha pulling back up, so he

knows they have to hurry up and get the fuck out

of there. Mack grabbed the nine millimeters and

hit that nigga Cash straight in the dome. The nigga

is dead before he realized that he shot.

Chapter 17

Mack instantly waves Tasha over. She jumped out of the car as if he'd called her. Tasha ran over, sees Jay bleeding. She knows it is not the time to ask questions. Tasha understands and respects the lifestyle Mack lives. Tasha helped get Jay in the backseat of Mack's car. Tasha even sat back there with her as Mack sped off heading to the rehabilitation center that Dallas set up.

Jay is drifting in and out. "Tasha keep her awake," Mack yelled.

Tasha begin talking to her. "Are you okay?" she asked as Jay leaked blood on her Prada dress.

Dallas picked up the phone. "Jay's hurt bad make sure a muthafucka is there to save her life nigga," Mack yelled.

Jay told Tasha, "I'm not going to make it." Tasha doesn't know what the fuck to say to the lady she'd just met.

"Hold on love. Please think of all the reasons you have to live." Jay thought of her mother, the trip her, Jasmine and Shannon take to Jamaica, her baby brother, Shannon's daughter and Jasmine's kids. Jay doesn't want to miss them growing up. She wanted to see her little brother graduate. Jay doesn't want her mother to have to bury her behind this. So she prayed for God to keep her.

Tasha then yelled at Mack, "Floor this muthafucka get her to some help! This woman is not about to fucking die in my arms!" Tasha hates to see the lady's life slipping away. She wondered what made this woman choose a job like that anyhow. Then it dawned on her; the same way she had been using her body to get by.

Tasha thoughts are broken by Mack opening the door to the car. There are women dressed in nurse scrubs with a hospital gurney. They got her on the table immediately checked her vitals making sure she is alive. Then they placed the IV in, hung the bag, and rushed Jay inside. Tasha can breathe easy because Jay is still fighting. It told her Jay has reason to live.

Dallas walked up to Mack as the three of them entered the building. He hadn't called anyone because he doesn't want to work the team up before he knows what is going on. "What the fuck happened to her man?" Dallas asked forgetting Tasha is there.

"Man all I know is that nigga Cash was in her car talking shit to her while she is slumped over in her car. He fired shots through the window," Mack told him.

"What were you doing there?" Dallas needs to know.

"Jay was parked in front of my damn apartment. I hadn't made it home yet because I went to pick up Tasha." Mack pointed to her.

Tasha is standing there quietly. She knows to stay out of men's business. Her mother taught her a woman should be seen not heard. So she just dressed to impress and spoke when spoken too. Tasha did what she is told to do by most men.

Dallas looked at the beautiful woman wondering why the hell she is there, but he knows that Mack had no choice but to bring her. "Did you get the nigga?" Dallas needs to know if the dude is handled or got away.

"The grim reaper got him," Mack assured him. Tasha smiled. She knows what that meant. It is a nickname that the streets gave Mack because he was known for sending a muthafucka to meet their maker.

"My nigga." Dallas bumped shoulders with him. Then Mack grabbed Tasha by the waist and said, "My baby helped me get this shit done." Dallas is shocked the nigga even had a bitch with him. For him to call her baby and praise her for helping is interesting.

"Is that right Ms. Tasha? It looks like we owe you a new dress but we're gonna throw in enough for some red bottom shoes and a Prada bag." Dallas smiled at her. She is excited to get that kind of money and not have to sleep with anyone.

Tasha is about to thank him when the nurse came running out. "She needs a blood transfusion," she stated.

"Give her one Tiffany," Dallas said.

"It's not that simple. Jay is O positive. We can't give her any other blood type but O positive. They can give to anyone, but can only take in O positive blood," Tiffany schooled him.

"Damn, what are we gonna do?" Dallas shook his head. It is time to call the crew.

"I'm O positive," Tasha stated.

"You're willing to do that for us?" Dallas asked the mysterious woman.

"Yeah I will do that for you," Tasha informed him.

"Baby thank you." Dallas liked the lady and hoped that Mack is picking up on the quality of woman that he had. If he wasn't careful, he could miss out on the best thing that could happen to any man.

Tiffany grabs her. "Come on; we don't have time to waste boo." She knows that Jay is clinging on to what life she has left.

Dallas got on the phone called Dizzy first. He picked up half-asleep. "Yeah," he answered.

"Aye man, I'm gonna need you to get over here. Shit is all bad. Jay's shot and Mack brought her to the rehab center in time, but she needs a blood transfusion. We handled that but everyone needs to get here cause this shit with her is touch and go." Dallas ran it down for him.

"What the fuck happened to her man?" Dizzy asked him. Jasmine is laying in his arms wondering what the hell is going on. It doesn't sound right from what she could hear.

"Man just gets here I have to call Zane and the girls," Dallas told him.

"Jasmine's here with me so we will be there shortly," Dizzy assured him.

"See you in a second family." Dallas ended the call. He dials Zane's number, and Shannon picked up.

"Who the fuck is this calling this bitch this fucking early?" Dallas smiled.

"Baby I need you guys to get here. Jay shot," Dallas told her.

"What the fuck! How did she get hit? I just fucking left her." Shannon was pissed. She was not about to let that shit ride.

"Don't stress just get Z up and get the fuck over here. She's hanging on, but we don't know if she is gonna make it or not yet," Dallas informed her.

"FUCK," Shannon yelled causing Zane to wake up.

"What's the matter, love? You in pain?" It scared him to think his baby might be harm.

"Jay's shot. We've got to get to the fucking rehab center. They don't know if she's gonna make it or not." Shannon is getting dressed and crying at the same time.

"FUCK," Zane yelled and hopped out of the bed to get ready as well. He is glad his little stepdaughter is still at her grandmother's house. Shit has just gotten real whoever did this shit is going to pay with their muthafuckin life.

Chapter 19

They pulled up to the warehouse. Nisha is feeling good about what she has done. The moment Shannon leaves him, he would be love sick all over again, and she would be there to pick up the pieces and talk him into skipping town with her. Zane wouldn't have to worry about the kids or anything because they are staying with her mom. She had already given her some money for them because she needs some alone time.

Shannon hopped out of the ride like she isn't pregnant at all. Zane saw her do it heads for the door. He held it open as she walked through and he let it go when he sees Nisha coming. The door hit her

"Damn Zane you didn't fucking see me coming," Nisha bitched.

"I did, I don't hold the door open for other niggas women." Zane put an "s" on nigga because she loves the crew.

"Don't fucking play with me. You weren't saying that shit last night." That statement caused the whole room to turn their heads.

"What the fuck happened last night?" Jasmine asked like Zane is her man. Shannon doesn't budge Mack watched her. He loves Shannon's G code. He could tell that she has this shit all in the bag.

"Jasmine sit your ass the fuck down. Why you in somebody else's damn business? We should be asking you and Dizzy about last night." Mack just wanted to start some shit because he knows what Shannon and Zane have is real. Shannon will get to the bottom of it all. Mack knows that Zane would never fuck with a bitch like Nisha.

"Mack stays the hell out of my business," Dizzy chimed.

"It's good baby," Jasmine stated.

"Baby," the whole room yelled.

Mack, Shannon, and Zane are dying laughing. Nisha is even more pissed. "Oh so everybody's just hooking up in this bitch," she stated.

"Too bad don't nobody want your stinky breath ass." Mack was clowning when Dallas and Tasha walked in the room.

"I am glad you have all the niggas chasing you down but please let them know that I am the top muthafuckin dog," Dallas stated as he entered the room with Tasha tailing him.

"What the fuck does that mean Dallas?" Nisha is over all the bullshit. She is her fucking boss. Hell Dallas isn't even the real boss. He answered to some bitch but wanted to flex with her.

"Pick up the damn phone when I call your stupid ass. It's not as I call you just to pass the time of day. When I call it's business and business only lady," Dallas assured her.

Nisha is pissed because she feels that Dallas is clowning because he has his bitch with him. Yeah, most would say she is bad, so he was trying to show out. "Whatever! Don't be acting a fool because you brought your bitch to work today. What is it brings my bitch to work day? Didn't nobody tell me." Nisha sat in one of the chairs after talking all her shit.

"Excuse me boo, I ain't no bitch or whore, so I must have shown up on the wrong fucking day." Tasha checked Nisha.

"FYI that's my bitch," Mack stated the whole damn room including Dallas is in shock.

Tasha smiled because she knows that she has finally gained his trust. Tasha loved that fool. She walked over and kissed him. "Like he said, I'm his bitch." Tasha is grinning from ear to ear.

"Not only is she that, but she's also family. Tasha helped save Jay's life not even knowing who the hell Jay is. When we almost lost Jay because we didn't have her blood type Tasha came in handy again, so I gave the sister much love and respect. If there anything that we can do, please let me know," Dallas told her.

"Can I work for the rehab center? I'm a nurse but can't find a job and would love to help you," Tasha said.

"I don't see why not," Dallas told her.

"Mack is it okay?" Tasha asked.

"You don't need my approval. You earned this boo." Mack has always been sweet on Tasha but after recent events, he would be a fool not to act like it.

"You're my man anything and everything I do I want it to be okay with you. When you were supposed to be dead, I knew you weren't because I felt you. Then I found you were in the hospital, but I just watched you from afar. You are the man for me, so please tell me if this ok or not." Mack looked at Zane, Dizzy, and Dallas like did you all hear that shit?

The three men mouthed, "Pimp on," and laughed.

"Baby you can work here, but your boy is paid so you don't have to. If you need my approval, the answer is yes. But will you do something for me?" Mack asked.

"Anything." Tasha was willing to die for that nigga.

"When I get back from this mission, marry me." Mack shocked his damn self. A bitch like this one he had nothing to lose and everything to gain.

"Yesssssssssssssssssssssssssssssssssssssss," Tasha screamed. "I finally got your ass. All my friends said that you were crazy and didn't want me, but I knew that hard work and love would win you over. I can't believe it," Tasha talked and cried. "I have to call my mother and tell her the great news." Mack laughed.

"She doesn't know me." He thinks Tasha is crazy but so is he.

"Oh but she does, she does." Tasha kissed him, chatted on the phone with her mother, and then heads to the nurse's area to claim her job as the head nurse in that bitch. She has finally found her home.

"Where you find the Mary Poppins of the Hood?" Nisha asked. That bitch's hate level was on a thousand.

"Not in your mother's sorry ass pussy," Mack stated, and the room busted out laughing.

"I'm happy for you bruh. She's beautiful, and she saved my girl's life, so she's all that to me," Shannon told him.

"Thanks, sis. It was you and that nigga over there that inspired a nigga like me to do this shit. So you have to help me I might fuck something else, but I won't leave my wife." Mack is honest, and Shannon shook her head.

"It's fresh baby if you slip up and fuck something else, but if the bitch every gets bold and show her head she dead cause she just wants what I got. You would never just cheat. These whores are just pressing you to do it hard so to get them off your back." Tasha kissed him.

"Thank you for understanding a nigga like me, baby." Mack kiss.

"They crazy as hell," Dallas said the room filled with laughter again.

Chapter 20

Jay is sitting up when Tasha came in the room. Three weeks have passed, and she is doing well. Jay is ready to get out of that bed and on with her life now that Cash is finally dead. He tripped her out because it seemed if she would have just loved him he would have forgiven all and rode off in the sunrise with her. She couldn't lie Jay didn't like him. She was doing her job, and there is always a price to pay when you fucked over people.

"How are you feeling Ms. Jay?" Tasha asked her. She has the place running smoothly. All the other nurses are glad to have her around to organize shit.

"I'm great. When I can get up out of here?" Jay asked she needs to water her plants.

"Today. You all right girl. I'm coming to let you know that Shannon brought you some clothing, and they're about to have some meeting that I can't go to in thirty minutes. You might want to get dressed and be there." Tasha hands her the clothing.

Jay hopped out of the bed like she hadn't been shot in the shoulder and on her side right under her rib just missing her lungs. She took the clothing and stared at Tasha. "Why?" Jay asked.

"Why what girl?" Tasha is hoping that she isn't fucking around with Mack.

"Did you save me? You don't know me like that so tell me why you did it." Jay needs to know.

"When I was young my mother got in some shit like this. She robbed a man, and he caught up to her with me in the car. He shot her three times not because he was mad about what she took but because she didn't love him. I could tell the man that hit you was angry for the same reason. My mother died in my arms, and I have been out here all alone all this time. I wasn't gonna let you die in my arms or at all for that matter. I was too young to save my mother, but God placed me here to save you, so that's why." It has nothing to do with Mack. It was personal for Tasha.

Jay laid the clothing on the bed and hugged her. "You will never be alone from here on out. You're my sister. We have the same blood running through us. Thanks to you I am alive." Jay hugged her.

"Sis you better get dressed and get to that meeting. You know how Dallas can be." Tasha hasn't been around long, but she has already learned to stay out of Dallas's way sometimes.

"Fuck Dallas," Jay stated as she went to get dressed. "Nobody scared of his shit-talking ass."

Tasha laughed she loves the crew. The women are just as gangsta as the men. Beautiful women, it spoke volumes to her. The love they shared for each other is unheard of in the hood.

The love that Nisha showed is the hood love she knows, but what the rest carried is something different, and she is honored to be a part of it.

Dallas walked past Shannon and Zane. He could tell they are debating something serious. It doesn't stop him from fucking with them. "Y'all going through something." He laughed.

"Man, go head on with that," Zane stated. Dallas laughed some more cause when Zane is pissed that is his favorite line. Dallas walked off letting them have their moment before the meeting started.

"Let me get this shit straight. Nisha told you that I am checking for her? No, let me say what you said, trying to fuck her." Zane can't believe that trifling whore is trying to play games.

"Yes!" Shannon acted as if she believed her but she doesn't.

"I came home and fucked the shit out of you," Zane states thinking how could she believe that.

"You were ok, but it wasn't all that." Shannon fucked with his ego.

"Bitch… Shannon if you weren't pregnant I would slap the shit out of you for lying." Zane is hot.

"Bitch nigga it wasn't all that don't get mad at me." Shannon knows that she is wrong, but she wanted to see how mad he is going to get.

"Oh, it wasn't?" Zane grabbed her by the collar pulling her into the other room.

"Let me go boy." Shannon wiggled.

Zane slammed the door once he had her in the chamber. She is wearing a V-neck tee and jogging pants. He ripped the shirt off her and yanked the pants down. "What are you doing?" Shannon hit him, but he doesn't care.

"Shut the fuck up." Zane is piss at Nisha.

Shannon is fighting. When he begins to kiss her neck, her pussy became wet. He worked his way down sucking on her nipples. "Ohhh." They were tender due to the pregnancy.

"Ohh what?" Zane asked.

Shannon doesn't say shit. That nigga had worked his way down to her pussy. He is sucking, slurping, and nibbling on her clit and she is losing her mind. Trying to be quiet. "Zane nnnnoooooooooooooooo don't do me like this," she yelled. The crew in the other room is wondering what was going on.

Zane came up and placed his dick into the wet pussy like he heard nothing she said. He fucked her hard but gently. "I didn't fuck you right because I wanted to fuck Nisha. Is that what you said?"

"I wassssssssssssss oooh ahh aaaaaahhhhhhh talking shiiiiiiiiiiittttttt. Omg," Shannon yelled.

"This what you get for talking shit. Now take this dick. Take this dick." Zane held her waist as he dug deep inside of her.

"I Mmmmm mmmm sooorrrrrrrrrryyy!" Shannon stated. She has to think of something to make that nigga bust.

"You damn right you are." Zane was dicking her down.

"Oooooohhh daddy you right. I fuccccccked upppp pllleassssee come for me daad DDD Dy." Shannon knows that shit would get hit.

"Ooooooohhh bitch you play dirty but that's why I loooooooveee your assssss." Zane was about to come.

"I ammmmm sooorrrrry BBB babby yy." Shannon's body is shaking like a fool.

Zane came with her. He kissed her and put his dick back in his jogging pants. "Now that's how you know that I don't want no other bitch but you. I just fucked the shit out of you." Zane begins to dance on her ass. Shannon is screwed up. She is still trying to catch her breath.

Chapter 21

Dallas came knocking at the door. Zane tossed Shannon a cover and opened the door. "What's good bruh?" Zane asked as if he doesn't know why he is at the door. Tasha us standing there too.

"Shit you tell me?" Dallas smiled.

"Nothing had to make my wife understand I am not to be fucked with. You ready for this meeting?" Zane walked out of the room.

Dallas laughed. "Yeah, boss." Shaking his head and looking at Shannon who was still out of breath.

"Tasha." The bass in Zane's voice made her jump.

"Yes, sir." Tasha is shaken up.

"Get her some scrubs so she can clean herself up." Zane licked his lips still tasting Shannon on them.

"Oooookay." Tasha knows why the woman here loved these men because the dick game in that bitch is insane.

Dizzy, Zane, Jasmine, Dallas, and Mack were sitting in the new conference room at the round table when Jay walked in. All of the conversation stopped. They didn't know that she was well enough to make the meeting or the mission.

"What the fuck is up with Y'all?" Jay asked noticing that she doesn't see Shannon or Nisha.

"Hey, Jay!" They are all glad to see her. They welcomed her with hugs.

"Where are Shannon and Nisha?" Jay wants to see them.

"We're giving Nisha ten more minutes to show her face in here." Dallas is tired of waiting on her.

"Shannon is in there asleep. I had to put her ass to bed," Zane stated.

"Zane don't play with my muthafuckin sister," Jasmine fussed at him.

"Aye your sister gonna learn that I am a muthafuckin man, and my word is my bond," Zane yelled. Jay doesn't know or care what they are fussing about; she is just glad to be back to see it.

Dizzy grabbed Jasmine because she is punching Zane. "Punk you don't run nothing." She likes Zane, but he is too cocky with his dick game.

"Aye, you better get her before she gets fucked up." Zane is using his arms to cover his head. Knowing that he was going to hit her.

"Baby ladies don't act like that," Dizzy told her.

"You're right!" Jasmine tried to bring it together.

Jay is shocked by the actions of Jasmine and Dizzy. Mack yelled, "She ain't no damn lady."

Jay is laughing. "I don't know what the hell you're laughing at. The next time you're getting your ass whooped and almost killed don't park on my damn street. Fucking with you, I got a whole wife now. Did you hear me? I went from being single to married all behind your ass?" Mack talked big shit but is loving Tasha more and more each day.

"You're lucky to have a bitch like her bastard," Jay told him.

"Look I ain't no bastard! Don't be calling my mama no whore." Mack is a fool.

"Nigga get the fuck out of my face." Jay laughed at his stupid ass.

Dallas sat watching them a wondering how he was going to walk away from his crew. He doesn't think he had what it takes to do it. What would be the reason for them to get together and act a fool? He is sad about ending it all. Dallas is going to talk to the boss about them pressing on. Why stop now?

As Dallas is sitting, watching his crew his phone began to ring. He looked at the phone and smiled. "Hey, white girl Kim." He often called her that just to drive her crazy because her body screamed sister.

"Dallas kiss my ass," Kimberly told him.

"Gladly it's been awhile." Dallas hates that he fucked things up between them.

"Whatever. I just called to let you know that Venom and I will be in town. She has to be with the police and ID the body. Since you don't know how to keep your city quiet." Kimberly hit a nerve.

"Don't do that shit Kim. You know I handle mines." Dallas hates for his gangsta to be questioned.

"Stop calling me white girl Kim then." She laughed.

"Thank you for the heads up boo." Dallas blew her a kiss through the phone.

"Whatever." She hung up knowing that she has a soft hot spot for that man. Hell, she had an itch. She puffed her blunt thinking she might let him scratch it. She looked over at Eric the new young cop lying in bed with her. He is no Dallas, but he would do. She leaned back, opened her legs, and said, "Eat." He does just as she demanded. Kim smoked and enjoyed the treatment

Chapter 22

Dallas is ready to get the meeting started yet Nisha has still not made it there yet. He doesn't know what the fuck she is on, but she is going to pay for playing games. It is not the time for that shit. He just has to get things moving along. It is time to punch the clock again, and nothing or one would hold the team back.

Everyone is sitting around chatting since Dallas is on an urgent call. They were all laughing and joking. It is good to see Jay back in good health and hanging with the crew. Dallas got off the phone. "Hey Y'all let's get this show on the road," he said grabbing their attention. "Well Nisha still hasn't come yet," Mack said knowing that she is on some bullshit.

"Fuck her we have to get down to business. We can't allow her to hold us up." Zane knows that Nisha would pay for playing games for real. She needs to pay for coming to his wife about him coming at her like that when she was the one trying to fuck him.

"Y'all know we are going to Vegas, and this is supposed to be our last mission," Dallas told them hoping that Venom would be cool with him and his team still hanging around.

"Supposed to be?" Mack is geeked up. He isn't ready to give up the life just yet.

"Don't get excited yet nigga it's just a thought," Dallas told Mack.

"Man this why I love this nigga. Alright, go ahead, do your thing boss." Mack is feeling good.

"As Y'all know we're going to Vegas this trip," Dallas stated.

"We?" Zane asked. He couldn't remember that last time that Dallas did a lick with the crew.

"Yes, nigga I'm going too. Don Q thinks me and him are about to link up together on some business type shit. Plus, I'm always looking for new hoes that want to get down," Dallas assured them.

"I'm glad you're riding out with us," Mack said.

"Yeah I got to see my boy put in work," Jasmine said.

"That nigga nice with that hammer saved a nigga's life a few time in the field," Dizzy informed them.

"Don Q owns the Lucky Horse, Slot Land, and Ace of Spade's Casino. He also has Deluxe Divas and Stallion's strip clubs. I don't give a fuck about the clubs. That's bullshit money. Plus, he thinks I want to buy the Lucky Horse, but the real truth is I want the deed to all three ya dig." Dallas smiled knowing that he is going to have to fuck that nigga Don Q over to get what he is after.

"I'm with that just tell me what the hell I have to do," Zane stated.

"Don Q ain't no lightweight niggas been trying to get at him for some time now. He's a heavy hitter and ain't willing to take no shorts. The nigga is always on point. He's only allowing me because he thinks we're friends. The only friends I have are in this building at the moment. Understood?" Dallas liked what he saw when he looked at their faces. Everyone there is willing to die but ready to live at all times.

"Indeed," Zane stated.

"I'm with it," Mack said.

"This the only family I have ever had," Dizzy reminded him.

"It's the only family I have left," Jasmine said thinking about her loss.

"I almost died for this," Jay said letting him know there is no turning back.

"Bravo! Whew, I haven't seen a team this strong in a while," Venom said, and the room froze. The ladies don't know who she is, but the men do. Kimberly's sneaky ass stated that they were coming not that they were fucking there already. Dallas would deal with her later.

Dallas walked around the room to greet Venom. He is in love with that woman. She had a husband that would bury him twelve feet deep if thought the nigga is checking. He smiled remembering when he met her. It is right before she found out the Vicious was her twin sister. He was down with the crew she had. The one that was causing havoc on Vicious shit, not knowing they were playing with the devil going up against that woman and her crew. Even though she had punk ass niggas on her team, she still came strong when she found out that he was against her.

Venom had her team but unlike others that got put on and left their crew behind, she cut from the same cloth as her sister. Loyalty is everything to them. She helped Dallas and the men get started by giving them the front money and managing the whole operation. She just didn't want to be the face of the shit. She plays her part in the cut.

Dallas stepped to her. "Where's Mello?" Dallas asked with a smile.

"He's at home, but his eyes are always on me," Venom assured him.

Dallas stepped to Kim. "Kim babe, happy to see you." Kimberly waved him off knowing that she wanted to fuck the shit out of him right then and there.

"Oh Y'all acting like that today," Dallas said as he introduced her to the ladies.

"This is Tasha. Mack's girl and head nurse here." She followed Venom and Kimberly into the office.

"Dallas I tried to stop her, but she wouldn't listen," Tasha informed him.

"Tasha when you see this woman move the hell out of her way and let her do what she pleases." Dallas schooled her.

"I'm sorry." Tasha held her head down.

Venom smacked the shit out of her. Tasha is shocked. "Don't apologize for doing your job, and you're a little off your job. Since you don't know me, and I am on your list, you were supposed to kill me. Get a backbone; men don't like a weak woman." Venom put her up on game.

At that moment, Tasha is pissed she smacked the shit out of Venom right back. "Is that enough fucking backbone? If you ever hit me again, I will kill you." Tasha is quiet, did as she asks, but far from a punk.

Venom shakes her head and smiled. "Great job Mack. My kind of bitch she's alright with me." Venom hates cowards.

Chapter 23

Mack's dick is so hard he is about to bust right there on the spot. He didn't know that Tasha could be that gangsta. He is most definitely fucking the shit out of her that night.

"Ms. V what's up with the drop by? Nigga couldn't get a text message or nothing?" Zane hugged and kissed her as he asked.

"Boy, you are still fine." Venom shakes her head.

"Yes he is and who are you?" Shannon came in the office.

Venom laughed. She had heard a lot about the Spitfire that has locked Zane down. "I am Venom, pleased to meet you, Shannon," she stated.

"Likewise but like I asked; who are you again?" Shannon didn't know her.

"I am the boss if you must know. All of this is stemmed from me and my sister Vicious," Venom told her.

Shannon smiled because she has heard of the famous twins that ran the city but had never seen either of them. She is impressed Venom is a bad bitch for sure. "Honored to meet you," Shannon said and hugged her like they were old friends.

The crew is talking amongst themselves. They had forgotten all about the meeting that had taken place until Nisha walked in Tasha let her pass. She knows who she is but doesn't care too much for her. She decided to stay out of Nisha's way because she doesn't want to fuck things up.

"I'm sorry I'm late. I was shopping, and you know how women can be when we're up in the mall," Nisha chimed as if she is a Hollywood star or something.

Dallas just shook his head. Kimberly doesn't know who she is, but Venom is very familiar with her. "Dallas what time did this meeting start?" Venom asked.

"At noon," Dallas informed her.

"What time is it now?" Venom needs facts before she spoke on shit.

"3:30, so that means she's three and a half hours late." Mack rubbed the shit in. Nisha side-eyed him but most of all she wants to know who the bitch is questioning her.

"Who the hell are you?" Nisha asked. Venom remembered this is the same smart-mouthed bitch from when she was on the phone.

"I spoke with you over the phone big mouth." Venom refreshed her memory.

"Oh, you're Dallas's boss." Nisha is cute.

"This bitch has a death wish huh?" Mack asked Zane.

"Looks that way," Zane said.

"No. I'm the boss of every muthafucka in this room little girl. I don't know how you got this job, but bitch I can tell you are way under qualified," Venom checked her.

"You are not my boss bitch I have never met you." Nisha is dumb as hell.

"Let me tell you something bitch," Venom said, about to charge her, when Kimberly grabbed her.

"Sis we didn't come here for this, and I think it's time we go. Dallas, we will be back around dinner time." Kimberly knows that shit is about to get real.

"Dallas this is the last mission right?" Venom asked.

"Yeah but I want to talk to you about that," Dallas told her. Mack is praying she agreed.

"I'm willing to hear you out, but no matter what we decide after this mission, I want you to get rid of this bitch," Venom spat.

"Get rid of me? I can leave it's nothing," Nisha mouthed off.

"Ughhhhh let me whoop her ass." Venom is wiggling in Kim's arms.

"Kim take her out I will handle it," Dallas assured them.

Kimberley got Venom out of there. She loves her short-fused friend, but she could be very dangerous at times. She knows some food, good green, and a drink would fix her up. They would come back and see Dallas later that night.

Dallas waited until she was gone before he spoke. "Nisha baby, I'm just gonna tell you that you're barking up the wrong fucking tree. That lady put all this together. Just because you weren't informed about that doesn't make it any less real. I can tell you this; you would rather have God on your bad side then this woman. She has no soul, and she will take yours." Dallas's words caused chills to run down Mack's spine.

"Well fuck it then! She said get rid of me, so I am out, right?" Nisha asked.

Dizzy laughed. "Nisha baby, you know all the dirt we have done. So don't get excited about that get rid of you statement cause it sure as hell won't involve you walking away from this shit," Dizzy schools her.

"Kill me? So you're gonna kill me, Dallas?" Nisha is pissed and scared.

"The meeting is over we will have another one in two days. At that time, we will talk about the decision Venom, and I made in regards to the crew," Dallas said as if she didn't ask him shit.

"Really? You're not gonna answer me," Nisha yelled.

"Nisha I hope to see you on time at the next meeting." The way Dallas said that it made the hair stand up on the back of her neck.

Chapter 24

The crew is leaving the warehouse. Jasmine

has not been in the best mood. She has been

staying at Dizzy's crib for the past few days.

Jasmine missed her husband but misses her

children more. Jasmine loved sleeping in Dizzy's

arms even though he refused to make love to her.

She is still enjoying the attention. He knows that it

would never be right if he fucked with her while

she was married.

Dizzy know that he couldn't allow that

woman to sleep in his bed and not fuck her for

much longer. It is time to put an end to the

madness before he fucked around and did some

shit that couldn't be undone. If he fucked her, she

would not be returning to her husband. He knows that he has to handle that shit fast as he stands in the hall hugging Jasmine in his arms.

"Jasmine," Dizzy said.

Jasmine pulled away from his embrace to look him in the eyes. "What's up Dizzy?" she asked even though his eyes already told her.

"Babe it's time for you to shit or get off the pot," Dizzy informed her.

She knows what that meant, but is hoping that she wouldn't have to deal with it until after the mission. Now that Dallas is speaking of not ending the crew, she doesn't know what to do because she can't walk away from it like that. "Do I have to do it now?" Jasmine asked because she isn't ready to be home alone, and she knows that Korey wouldn't come back or give her the children as long as she is living that life.

To be honest, that life isn't safe for her family. Jasmine doesn't want to be selfish, but what could she do if she had to choose.

"Yes, the time is right. If that man loves you like he says he does, he will do one of two things. He'll accept what you're doing or love you enough to let you go. It's just that simple. You have to decide if this is worth what you already have. I will tell you now if God were into making deals I would trade all this shit I'm doing to get my wife and my baby back. I don't have that option, but right now, you do. As sexy as you are, I don't want to let that get in the way of what's right." Dizzy is a man on every level.

"Damn, you're right. Fuck! Why aren't you the kind of person that just takes the pussy and doesn't care?" Jasmine needs to know because most niggas didn't care.

"Look around boo most of the niggas in here are looking for one thing more valuable than money, and that's love. We can grind yet not know who we can trust. Is it lust or money they want out of us? So when you find a great thing you hold on to it. That's why I'm not going that route with you, cause once I grab hold, I am never letting go," he schools her.

Jay came out just as the two is finished talking. "Jasmine you ready to roll?" She could see the chemistry that Jasmine and Dizzy shared.

"Yeah, sis. You're ready I see." Jay is holding her side. The pain meds are wearing off. She needs to get home to take the pain pills and sleep because she isn't going to miss out on that mission for anything in the world.

"Yeah this pain is kicking my ass, and I've got to rest up for the mission." Dallas is headed to his car past them and heard the conversation.

"You're not going, Jay. It's way too soon," Dallas said.

"Yes, the fuck I am going. Dallas, you're the boss, not my damn daddy. I will be well enough to do my fucking job. Nothing or no one will stop me. The only fucking way I am missing the mission is if I'm dead, and I feel alive right now," Jay barked.

Dizzy and Dallas are shocked that she came off so strong. "Jay I am not for the bullshit. You heard what I said, and that's final." Dallas jumped in the car and peeled off.

"Final my ass," Jay yelled at him knowing that he couldn't hear her due to the surround sound he has in his car. She looked at Jasmine. "Bitch let's go he's got me fucked up," she said getting in the car.

Jasmin kissed Dizzy on the cheek. "Thank you." She walked to her car, and he waved and blew her a kiss as she pulled off. Mack came out to see him waving he shakes his head, "Yo ass still ain't fucked her," Mack teased.

"Not because I couldn't, but cause I'm a classy nigga." Dizzy popped his collar and laughed.

"I'm glad I'm ratcheting because I fuck the shit out of bitches," Mack stated.

"Nigga ain't you about to get married?" Dizzy can't believe this nigga. Those bullets that left in him made him crazier than he was.

"Yeah what's that mean?" Mack asked him like he is stupid.

"Nothing nigga, nothing." Dizzy hopped on his motorbike and ride out.

Chapter 25

Nisha is pissed. She can't believe that Venom had told Dallas to kill her. If she had known that he was down with Vicious and Venom, she would have never joined him. Like she had a choice to get with him. Dallas had kidnapped her planning to kill her, so she had decided to save her ass versus West's. She didn't love West any fucking way. Nisha is about self and getting what she needed for her and only her. Nisha doesn't give a fuck about the other woman that are on their team. She just needed the extra hands to get the job done.

Nisha has somewhat smartened up and isn't spending money like she is crazy. She is holding about a hundred and fifty thousand after giving her mother fifty thousand to take care of the kids while she skipped town. Nisha is heading to Vegas in search of Don Q. She knows that if Dallas is on him, he wouldn't be hard to find.

Dallas should have known not to trust a bitch that is willing to set up a nigga that she was sleeping with for over a year. Some shit would come back and bite you in the ass. Nisha is preparing to bite the hand that has been feeding her. It could cost her life, but she doesn't give a fuck at the time. She isn't going to be disrespected by anyone at all. In Nisha's mind, she started the shit, and if it weren't for the crew that turned on her, Dallas wouldn't be shit.

Nisha is packing her bags and getting ready to make her moves. She isn't ever coming back to the Lou. She would send for her children once she handled all the shit that she has gotten herself into.

Nisha is taking Mega Bus because it's low key, and flights often get you caught up. She knows that she needed to move now because time was of the essence. Nisha can't let Dallas's team touch the city before her because then it would be too late for her to get the revenge that she is seeking.

Jay had made it home and taken the medicine that she needed. Her home feels foreign to her because she hasn't been there since the night that she fell out with Q. A part of her missed the hell out of him, yet she is glad that it is over with for the moment. She doesn't have to deal with the questioning behind being shot. Q would have been playing twenty-one questions about some shit that she is not allowed to speak of.

Jay is still a little tight about the fact the Dallas that just wanted to put her out of the mission like she was shit. That is bullshit to her. She is fine now, and he wanted to sit her down that go around. That is such an unfair act in her eyes. She had put in work and earned her stripes in that shit, and no one is going to take that away from her.

As Jay drifted off to sleep, she prayed that Dallas would change his mind. Whether he did or not she is still going so she just hoped that he had a change of heart. She couldn't accept the terms that he has set for her.

Shannon is sitting on the couch eating ice cream and cookies. She has been a bitch all day since she left the warehouse. She is feeling some way about not going in the field with her crew. In her condition, she isn't useful, and she knows that, but it doesn't make her feel better about the situation.

Zane could tell that her spirit is weak, and he hates that because she lashed out at everyone in the house when she was that way. He had put his stepdaughter down for a nap so that he could talk to Shannon about how she is feeling these days.

Zane sat down on the couch and asked, "Can I have some?" Zane smiled at her.

Shannon hates him because his smile brightened her whole world. "No." Shannon is still being mean.

"You are so stingy now fat mama." Zane teased her. He doesn't even want any for real; he just wants to make her smile.

"I am not! You're just asking to bother me. You don't eat this kind of stuff." Shannon let him know that she knows what he is on.

"Well since we know what this is about, let's talk," Zane said.

"There's nothing to say if you ask me," Shannon told him.

"I didn't ask you shit. I'm telling you because you've been bugging out for real," Zane called her on the bullshit.

Shannon didn't want to be bothered with it, but she knew that he wasn't going to let it go. So now was the time to put it all on the table. "Look at me." She stands and he could see the budding stomach that she had. It is cute to him, and he smiled again. "You are sexy to me," he assured her.

"Yeah I bet I am, but I ain't shit out there but another pregnant bitch that's waiting at home for a nigga to take care of her. I told myself that I would never let this happen to me again." Shannon paced the floor.

"What the fuck! Are you serious right now?" Zane asked.

"Yes, I am. I am that bitch. Me, and now look at this, I will be sitting out this mission," Shannon rants.

"If I had it my way you would be out of this shit all together. I'm not having my wife doing this crap to have to tell my kids that I buried her cause we were living a risky lifestyle." Zane was pissed.

"What the hell is the difference in me burying yo ass?" Shannon asked him.

"First, I am a man. Secondly, you will know what it is like to be loved by a real nigga, the right way, if the muthafucka after me can't fill these shoes. See the last nigga that you had is so lame that you don't know what a real nigga is about. Once I'm done loving you the nigga would have to be more than a billionaire to get your attention. That's the difference." Before Shannon could respond, he grabbed his car keys and slammed the door as he walked out. She sat back on the couch eating her ice cream as she cried. There is no way a man could love you that much.

Mack is lying in bed with Tasha. It blew his mind that he loved this woman. She is the first and would probably be only. Little does he know,

Tasha isn't going anywhere. She is there for life on some ole "Color Purple" type of shit. "Nothing but death would keep her from him." Tasha's honey brown skin is glistening from the small beads of sweat that laid upon it due the sexual workout she had given Mack. "I fucked the shit out of you," Tasha said catching Mack off guard.

"What?" Mack laughed, she is bugging.

"You know that I did daddy." She giggled.

Mack is thinking, "Yeah the girl is a beast in the sheets." He doesn't remember her doing it like that. If he had, he would have been wife her ass. "You got a few moves," he said and smiled.

"A few moves!" She grabbed his dick and began to lick it. Tasha moaned because she loved the way that man tasted. Hell, she didn't think that she would ever have any of his kids unless they came from swallowing.

Mack is enjoying that shit. His dick is still sensitive because it hadn't been long since his last nut. "Got damn T," he yelled because the bitch in him wanted to scream like a hoe.

"Call me Mama." Tasha swallowed him whole.

"Heeeeelllllllll nooo goooooo." He couldn't handle the shit that she was doing to him. The nigga's toes were already curling. He isn't about to call her no damn mama.

Chapter 26

Tasha's phone begins to ring, and Mack

think he is saved by the bell, but Tasha didn't come

up for air. She keeps sucking like her next meal

depend on it. "BBBaaaaabbbyyy yoohoo phon NN

EEE," Mack managed to say.

Tasha doesn't give a fuck about the phone,

but the knock at the door fucked it all up. She

knows that no one but the family knows where

Mack lives, so it is either a personal or business

visitor. She looked at Mack and smiled. "Get yo

ass off me." Mack hoped out of bed naked

wondering who the hell was at his door. Mack had

the hammer in his hand. He never asked who it

was at the door because if a nigga were coming for

his head, they wouldn't know if he there or not until the door opened, and they better be ready too because he is.

Mack opened the door aiming the heat at Zane. Zane pushed the heat out of his way walking past the naked Mack to see Tasha standing in the living room naked as well holding a sawed-off shotgun.

"I'm glad Y'all bare asses stay ready, but that's too much. Relax and get dressed," he ordered as he is in his house.

Tasha ran off to get herself together, and her damn phone is still ringing. It is her friend Meka calling. "Meka what do you want?" she asked.

"Oh a bitch gets a man, and she starts to act funny with her friends?" Meka is jealous and happy for her at the same time. She is glad that Tasha got the man she has craved all her life. She is jealous that she is still with the same sorry broke nigga that has given her five babies and hell all her life.

"Bitch you know I'm not like that, but I was enjoying my baby. That's all, but Mr. Sexy is here so we had to take a break," Tasha said that cause that's what Meka would call him whenever Mack came through with Zane to give her a little money. Meka never understood why he would give her money but not him. To Mack money isn't shit his heart is his lifeline he can't let anyone kill that.

"I understand, but I wanted to ask you what is that bitch's name on Y'all team that you don't like or trust?" Meka loves to gossip.

"Nisha." Tasha wonders why she cares.

"Yeah I thought so that bitch skinny thinks she's a real-life Barbie?" Meka wanted to be sure before she threw salt.

"Yeah, that's her. Why?" Tasha asked.

"She just boarded a Mega Bus going to a Vegas," Meka told her.

"What? Are you sure?" Tasha knew that bitch was dirty.

"Yeah, I just sold her the ticket." Tasha has forgotten that Meka started a second job at Mega Bus.

"Girl thank you. I owe you some money, but I have to go," Tasha told her. She doesn't know what Mack's next move is but she doesn't think that she should be holding the fact that Nisha skipped town to herself.

"Man she's bugging," Zane told Mack.

"Man you know how Shannon can be. She is a ball of fire the baby has her feeling some way. She is not the type to be kept, she keeps. A woman like that will not just lay down and let you take care of her. Hell, Tasha's here with a nigga, and I told her that she doesn't have to work her job at the warehouse. She said that even if she and I break-up she's not quitting. Ain't that a bitch?" Mack's ass is still bare and passing the blunt to Zane.

"Look, nigga, I don't like smoking with a naked nigga, only nude bitches, and yeah you have a point." Zane inhaled the smoke.

"Nigga this my house and I don't want you. I have a bad bitch in the next room; I am just comfortable with me. You're just mad cause my dick is bigger than yours." Mack talked his shit as he put on basketball shorts that were laying on the couch.

"Nigga, please. Don't let me get naked in this bitch; you won't have a wife anymore." Zane is cocky like that at times. He passed the blunt back to Mack.

"Man don't play like that I have a happy home." Mack is serious about something for a change, and it looked good on him.

"Damn, you're falling nigga I like it. I know how you feel my baby did me the same way. That's why I want to take her out of this life. Am I wrong for that?" Zane asked because he met her in that life.

"No, you not because these women should have never had to walk on this side of the world. Niggas are so bitch made that they had to do what they had to do. You've got to respect that." Mack is the smartest asshole Zane ever met in his life.

"That's why I fuck with you; man you keep it one thousand. Shannon has to sit this one out, but I pray I get to see the day she just walks around being the lady that God designed her to be." Zane sat back on the couch.

Mack prayed that they all would grow old together because even though he died, he still doesn't know what is on the other side. He remembered nothing about it all. All Mack know is that he is back, and he is going to try to get it right as best he could this time around.

Tasha came in the room in a floor length teddy. Her body is a plus sized coca cola bottle that screamed drink me. Zane loves all woman, and if you haven't been with a fat lady, Tasha will make you change your mind for sure. "Mack I just got a call from Meka…" Mack cut her off.

"Tell her ass no, not tonight you're not going out," Mack said shocking himself, but he wants her home with him. He would be leaving town soon, and it was not a guarantee that he would make it back.

Tasha giggled loving the love he has been showing her. "No baby, that's not what I wanted to ask. I was talking too much and told her that I didn't like or trust Nisha, and she called me to ask how Nisha look. I told her and she said that she just sold Nisha a bus ticket out of town." Tasha shakes her head thinking that Mack is going to be mad at her for the way she feels.

"What," Mack and Zane both yelled causing her to jump.

"I'm sorry," was all that Tasha could think to say. She begins to cry.

"Aye cut that shit out! You didn't do anything wrong so don't do that crying shit on me." Mack hates for a woman to cry. He would give a bitch anything just to keep the tears inside her head. Mack hugged her.

"Tasha baby does your friend know where she's heading?" Zane asked her.

"To Vegas." She sniffled.

Mack's eyes popped. "Baby go get my clothes and shoes," he told her. Tasha hurried to do what he asked.

"Shit just got real," Zane said Mack.

"I know that's why we've to get over to Dallas's house now. A phone call won't work in this case." Zane knows that Mack is right. He waited for the nigga to get dressed.

Chapter 27

Dallas is suited and booted in an Armani suit and all black Prada wingtips. He is looking perfect for the occasion. Kimberly and Venom come over to have dinner with him. He looked at Kimberley in her Vera Wang Black silk dress and black satin pumps. She is showing out tonight and Dallas is loving it! Venom is dolled up in an Ann Taylor silk jersey gown. A flowing cape gently cascaded from a halter neckline that is black as well.

The place looked like a palace. It caused Venom to smile because she remembered when she and Dallas were scrapping the bottom of the barrel for their next meal. Now their dinnertime meal looked like a Thanksgiving feast. No more sleeping in the hallways of the projects or on the home boys' sofa when you were lucky. Today the sky is the limit. They didn't get it the right way, but it is the only way they know. All they could do is pray that God understands the strong do what they have to survive.

"Dallas you're living like a king," Venom told him.

"A king? I don't know about that." Dallas sipped champagne.

"Please look at the home you built for yourself," Kimberley chimed. Hell, she is a detective, and her lifestyle is not like his.

"Yeah the home and money are right, but I am learning that a King is a royalty because he is surround by a family that loves and respect him. Look around; it's just me here," Dallas told them.

Venom couldn't deny that he is speaking the truth. She remembers when she joined with Vicious's team and started making money. When she bought her first house, she had no one to love. She was mad as hell and even a little jealous of her sister because she had the love that she needed and wanted in her life. Once she let Mello in all that changed, and Venom world is complete. "Dallas I have to agree with you on that one." She let him know that she feels him.

"Let's have some drinks and get away from this mushy shit." Dallas hates feelings.

The ladies laughed as they take their seats at the table. The waiter came in with Hennessey and Red Bull on the rocks. The room has smooth R & B playing. The environment is pleasant. "Dallas, what is it that you wanted to speak to me about?" Venom asked. Kimberly already has an idea of what it is.

"Venom we're not ready to call it quits yet, and it's not the money we're addicted to, it's the lifestyle," he told her.

"Well, my boy is not one hundred percent prepared to walk in these shoes so I will be here to hold his hand along the way. I also wouldn't mind having your team in my corner when I need you. Now, whatever money you make, it is what it is. I just don't want any dead bodies or heat brought to my city at all.

"I am always on your team and call when you need me. I'm usually not sloppy with how I handle business unless something unexpected happens like it did the other day. Had I known that dude was on the hunt for payback I would have gotten rid of him," Dallas assured her.

"Then you have my blessing to keep going as long as you see fit love," Venom told him, and Kimberly smiled.

"Don't be smiling sexy, you're not a part of this crew," Dallas teased Kimberley.

"Shit if I ain't nigga, much as I risk my ass for the team." Kimberley waved her hands and rolled her eyes as she talked. Dallas loved that she is so hood and never scared.

The waiter came in yet he has no food with him. "Mr. Dallas you have guests in the living room," he stated nervously.

Dallas knows that it isn't good if it called for unexpected people to come to his home. "Follow me," he told the ladies.

Zane and Mack are sitting on the couch. The looks on their faces said that shit is wrong. He isn't in the mood for bad news. Dallas wants to have a good night and get some pussy but the way that shit is looking, he knows that his night is not going to go as planned. "Why Y'all here?" he asked. He knows that sounded foul, but his boys understand the question.

"Nisha skipped town family," Zane told him.

"What the fuck?" Dallas can't believe that shit.

Venom shakes her head. "That bitch has to go."

"My wife's friend sold her a Mega Bus ticket, and she called and told her what was going down," Mack said Dallas.

"Where the fuck is the bitch going?" Venom asked.

"Vegas," Zane and Mack said at the same time.

"What? I know this hoe is not trying to give a heads up on my movement. I can't fucking believe this shit for real." Dallas is pissed beyond words.

"We're not sure, but that's what it looks like because what other reason would she have for heading that way," Zane said as he looked at his phone. Shannon is blowing him up, but she is going to have to wait.

"Fuck! Call everyone that's going. We move tonight. Hopefully, we will make it before she makes it to him," Dallas stated. Kimberley is pissed because she knows that the sexcapades that she had planned wouldn't happen this visit.

"What about Jay?" Mack asked. He had heard Dallas say she couldn't go.

"No. She's still hurt. I would have reconsidered if we had waited a few days, but now is just too soon," Dallas said.

That meant that Jasmine, Dizzy, Mack, Zane, and Dallas would have to handle it. Venom wants Nisha's head on a platter. "Do you need my hands?" she asked even though they haven't been dirty in years.

"No, you don't walk this walk anymore. Your husband would gun me down and kill me if I allowed that. Head back home and I will see you when I get back," Dallas assured her.

Venom respected what he said. "Kimberley let's head out mama because we might need you to get your Vegas police department friends to turn a blind eye to this shit." Venom kissed Dallas before heading for the door.

"I will get on it as soon as I get back to my office," Kimberley told her. She kissed Dallas as well.

Chapter 28

Jasmine is with her children. She has

decided that Dizzy is right. She is going to have to

deal with the task at hand. The kids were loving

her being there. They missed her so much. Korey

feels some way watching them with her. He missed

his wife, and Korey blamed himself for allowing

things to get that far out of line.

"Jasmine we can fix this if you want to,"

Korey told her because he isn't going to play

games.

"I have things that are unfinished, and you're

not willing to accept that are you?" she asked as

she hugged her only daughter.

"No, I can't say that I can. Jasmine this isn't our life. Look around," he told her.

"You're right this is my life." Jasmine knows it sounds selfish, but it is the truth.

"Got damn! We are your family, not them lazy fucks that would rather take than work for what they need." Korey is fuming.

"We put in hard work for more than a sorry ass two-week check," Jasmine told him. He would know if he let her give him some of the damn money but he has too much fucking pride.

"Get the fuck out of here! You call that shit work gangsta boo," Korey said as he gathered the kids to put them to bed.

Jasmine was about to speak when she saw Dizzy's number come across the phone. Jasmine knows that something is wrong when she picked up the phone. "Hey," she said.

"Get to the warehouse we are moving out tonight," Dizzy said as he got his car keys and headed for the door.

"What the fuck is going on? I'm here with my kids," Jasmine said.

"Nisha skipped town, and she's heading to Vegas," Dizzy told her as he as pulled out of the driveway.

"Fuck," Jasmine yelled. She can't believe that trifling ass bitch had pulled that.

Korey walked back in the living room wondering why she is screaming as he heard her say, "I will be there in thirty minutes. Jasmine hung up the phone and got up to gather her shit. "Where you going?" he asked as if he doesn't already know.

"I have to make a move," she said moving fast putting her shoes on.

"Jasmine, do me a favor?" Korey asked.

"What's that?" Jasmine knows he is on some bullshit.

"Don't come back here until you're done with this life. If you want to see the kids see them at school but I will let them know that you are not allowed to take them anywhere," Korey informed her.

"Whatever." She slammed the door on her way out. Jasmine doesn't have time to deal with the bullshit that he is throwing her. She would deal with all of it when she makes it back but right now duty calls, and she has to answer.

Dallas yelled, "Gas up the jet as soon as Jasmine and Dizzy get here, we're moving out." His line clicked, and he sees it is Don Q.

Dallas ends the call to see what the man knew so far. "What up fam," Dallas said playing the shit off.

"Nothing boy was seeing when you gonna touch down in my city," Dallas called him earlier telling that plans have changed and that he is coming to handle their business sooner.

"Waiting for my staff and then I am on the jet heading that way. I will check you in the morning so we can link up baby." Dallas remained calm.

"That's what I'm talking about a nigga that's ready to make that money, you heard me," Don Q told him.

"Yup you know it," Dallas said.

"In the morning nigga." Don Q ends the call.

Dallas sees Dizzy coming in. "Hey, family you ready to do this?" Mack asked him.

"Nigga I was born to do this," Dizzy stated on his hip shit lately.

"Is that right." Mack laughed.

"Aye, it ain't muthafuckin time to be playing and shit." Dallas is stressing. He has never had anyone turn on him like that. That shit has him bugging out badly.

"Man shut the fuck up. Whatever that bitch is going to do she is going to do. We're going to get what we after by any muthafuckin means necessary." Mack isn't about the bullshit he is on.

"Aye watch your fucking tone! I'm the boss in this bitch," Dallas reminded him.

"Act like it got dammit," Mack said.

Zane is on the phone with Shannon, telling her what is going down, and that he would be back in a few days. Shannon is pissed, but there is nothing she could do in the condition she is in but pray, so that's what she does silently.

Jasmine walked into all the bickering wondering what is going on. "Hey what the hell is Y'all fighting for?" Dizzy smiled.

"Don't worry about it just bring your slow ass on," Dallas said as they were heading to the jet.

"Dallas man I know you're stressing but watch how you talk to this lady," Dizzy checked him real fast Jasmine smiled.

"Ugh, damn not you too. These were all my bitches then Y'all started picking them off, and I have to watch my mouth and shit." Dallas fussed as they walked to board the jet.

"Damn right you do," Jasmine cosigned what Dizzy said. She is hoping that Dallas got a drink on the jet and chilled for the ride. They all

loaded up in the jet. It is do or die time.

Chapter 29

Don Q is sitting at his desk at the Stallion when Lola Bandz came in the office with the skinniest bitch that he had ever seen in his life. He doesn't know what the hell she is about to do up in there but it damn sure isn't working. Not if stripping is involved Lola Bandz is his main bitch. She is from up the way in Lancaster near Chicago. She has traveled there to dance. She wasn't making any money for real up there either.

Lola isn't that comfortable to the eyes. She reminds you of Whoopi Goldberg with a perm, but she is hard working and a hustler. Lola also thinks her suburban ass is gangsta and always putting work. She keeps the strippers in the place in check too. No bullshit, no short money, that bitch is money hungry, so Don Q kept her for himself.

"Lola what the hell is this woman back here for?" he asked because he knows that she know damn well better than to think this skinny heffa is getting on his stage.

"This is Nisha she told me that she came here from Saint Louis looking for you. Said that she has something you would want to hear," Lola said to him.

Don Q know that Dallas lived in the Lou, and he is hoping that nigga hasn't sent that bitch there for work because he didn't have any for her. "What is that you have that can help me and what do you want out of it?" Don Q know this is someone that is out for something.

"I'm a Duffle Bag Bitch, or I used to be, but I am tired of this life, and I can't do it no more. I'm here to give you the heads up on Dallas." Nisha knows the name rang a bell.

"Dallas huh? Have a seat," he told her.

Nisha sat down hoping that she doesn't get herself killed trying to give up the 411 on her team. "Dallas is going to rob you and take the deed to the Lucky Horse if not all your properties. I am supposed to be on that mission, but I have to wash my hands of this lifestyle. I have children you dig," Nisha rambled on.

Don Q can't believe the shit that he is hearing. He couldn't believe that nigga is about to put the moves on him. Yes, he knows what kind of business Dallas is into, but he never thought that he was a target. He thought it is just two businessmen linking up to handle some shit. Now this whore is up in there talking slick. He decided to call Dallas to see if he could get his vibe but nothing is off. This bitch is sitting there talking shit. Don Q doesn't know if she is a woman scorned or not but he is aware that those kind are the worst kind.

He is not about to jump the gun and call the man on some shit he isn't on. But he isn't going to be ambushed either, so he is going to put the squeeze on that bitch. "Nisha Dallas doesn't sound like he's up to no good to me, but you are looking like a rat right about now." He is irate.

"I'm not the one you have to worry about it's him and his crew. They will kill me when they find out I told you." Nisha begins fake crying.

"Even if it is the truth, what made you want to inform me? I know that you were down with the team putting in work so what's the deal, Ms. Lady?" Don Q doesn't trust hoes.

"Look I just got saved, and I wanted out, and they are threatening to kill me. I was hoping if I came here you could stop them," Nisha lies.

"You kill them right?" Don Q asked.

"Well yeah. If they have to kill you to get what they're after they will," Nisha told him.

"Hmm, why doesn't a godly woman like yourself let God and your faith handle this?" Don Q laughed.

"I trust in my Lord, but these people are monsters," Nisha told him.

"I don't believe you." A part of Don Q does.

"Ok, then I guess my help isn't needed here. I will just go, don't say that I didn't warn you." Nisha figured she would just keep it moving and head to Florida. Little does she know that shit isn't that simple.

"You can't go nowhere." Don Q gave Lola Bandz the head nod. Lola walked out of the room without speaking.

"What the fuck you mean I can't leave? I am a grown muthafuckin woman. Just like I walked in this bitch, I'm walking out." Nisha shakes her head from side to side, as she walked out.

"Bitch you sound just like a Christian," Don Q said calling her on her lie.

"Nigga I don't have to explain shit to you." Nisha heads for the door. Lola entered with two huge goons.

"Take her to the bay." Don Q had a dock where he went to get rid of muthafuckas that needed to take a long nap.

"They're not taking me nowhere. I don't belong to Y'all." Nisha tried to run past the goon and is knocked out cold. The other goon picked her up and heads out the door "Kill her?" Lola asked.

"No, not yet I don't know what this bitch is on or this nigga Dallas so just keep her in the room," Don Q told her.

"Anything for you baby," Lola said.

"Get out." Don Q isn't in the mood for all that love shit she is bringing his way. He hasn't had muthafuckas bring heat to him years, now here come this bullshit being placed in his lap.

Whatever is heading his way he isn't going out

without a fucking right because he worked his ass

off not asking any muthafucka for shit. Yeah, he

stunted hard, but he has every right to. That's why

he bragged about what he has so often. Because

growing up, he never had shit, not even parents.

So if that is what Dallas wanted, he is going

to have to take the shit, and he meant that. He laid

back in his chair and prayed she is lying.

Chapter 30

Dallas and the crew had touched down and checked into the Golden Nugget in the Rush Tower. They were supposed to stay at the Lucky Horse, but Dallas doesn't want to chance it if Nisha has beaten him there, so he switched shit up. They don't know that it is going to throw a red flag up to Don Q.

The crew all went to get rested up because they need all the energy they could get in the next three hours before it is time to move. If Nisha hasn't made it, they would have more time, but if she has, shit is going to go fast.

Dallas has talked to Kimberley, and she has handled the police thing, so he is good. All he has to do is get in and get out. Shit is never that easy, and Dallas knows that. As he stands in his room looking out the window at the view, he could see the Palms Hotel. Dallas enjoyed the view, but the lifestyle has taken a toll on him. He could walk away, but not everyone wants out, and a huge part of him would miss it as well. He doesn't want to stop; he just needs to slow down.

Don Q answered his call. "My nigga, you made it." He didn't let Dallas know Nisha is out there gassing.

"Yeah man I got jet lag like a muthafucka." They both laughed.

Don Q isn't a bad nigga, and Dallas has the money to buy him out, but he is just used to taking the shit, and some shit was die-hard. The shit is like a disease; it spread through your body faster than crack and caused you to be hooked on the life.

"You're at the Lucky Horse right?" Don Q asked.

"Man no my people wanted to stay at the Golden Nugget," Dallas lies.

"Hmm pass on three nights free for some exclusive shit. Y'all must be getting that paper in the Lou." Don Q is starting to think Nisha is right.

"You know young niggas want to stunt. You know about that shit you be on all the time," Dallas told him.

"Really huh? You think a nigga be on his show time shit?" Don Q is mad as hell but hiding it well.

"You don't be nigga?" Dallas asked him.

"Sometimes." Don Q laughed for good measure but isn't shit funny about what is about to jump around Vegas.

"I thought so nigga. I'm gonna lay it down and fuck with you in the a.m.," Dallas told him.

"Life or death right," Don Q said.

That made a light come on in Dallas's brain. "What the fuck you mean by that?" Dallas asked.

"Live or die to get this money nigga." Don Q played it off.

"Yeah." Dallas hung up.

He knows that Nisha is already there and talking so, he had to call the crew because they can't sleep in that place.

"Zane," Dallas said.

"What's real boss?" Zane asked him, and Mack is in the same room.

"Go to Jasmine and Dizzy's room. We're leaving; meet me in the lobby. Nisha's here and Don Q is on to us. We're still going to get him, but we can't let the nigga catch us with our pants down. You feel me?" Dallas schools him real fast.

"Say no more we're coming down. Where are we heading?" Zane asked.

"I know a little bitch that used to work the strip for me that lives here. We're gonna crash her shit," Dallas told him. He doesn't want to chance the hotels because if Don Q is smart, he will make a move while he thinks they are at the hotel sleeping.

Zane did what is asks of him. He is in his box about what happened and how Nisha is playing the game. That bitch better prays he doesn't find her before anyone else because he is going to erase her dog ass. That is one dog ass bitch. He shakes his head as heads to the lobby.

Don Q is sitting in his office while Lola walked back and forth like she is a mad woman. "So you're gonna let this nigga come to your home like that and think he's about to put the squeeze on you, babe?" Don Q loves her but sometimes the bitch talked too much.

"Lola I got this shit okay." He doesn't because he isn't prepared to go to war.

"I'm just saying if you had it that bitch wouldn't have had to come tell you a nigga you thought was your friend is about to shake you down like you're Bird. He is Big Red from the Five Heart Beats." Lola is always making movie references. Don Q hated when she did that.

"Lola shut the fuck up call Tommy Gunz and Big Nate. We're going to move on these niggas while they're sleeping. I have a lil bitch over at the

Golden Nugget that will get me in the rooms." Don Q is nervous.

"Ok don't let that little bitch over there get you fucked up. I can't believe this nigga Dallas just like that nigga Kane in Menace to Society," Lola stated.

"Lola stop doing that dumb ass shit and go fucking call them." Don Q slammed his hands on the desk.

"Doing what?" Lola asked.

"Making them damn movie references to everyday life." Don is fuming.

"What the fuck ever. Don't be coming for me because you don't love a nigga like Sunny did

Shame in Low Down Dirty Shame," Lola said

walking out of the room.

Chapter 31

Markita answered the door. She is a dark chocolate brick house. Not the small kind but the healthy significant to the world type. To men, she is to die for forty-four, thirty-six, forty-four. Hips and ass for days, weeks, months, and years. She is shocked to see Dallas on the other side of the door and that he isn't alone. She has mad love for him, though.

"Dallas what the hell are you doing here?" Markita smiles.

"Hey, baby! I have business here," Dallas told her.

Markita opened the door to let him in she knows he and the crew need to crash. Markita doesn't mind because Dallas is going to break her off with some paper.

Jasmine pushed past the men she is just glad to see another bitch. "Hey, I'm Jasmine I'm usually not this friendly, but these niggas are getting on my damn nerves, so I'm grateful to see another woman ya dig." Markita laughed because Jasmine makes her miss her home girls back in the STL.

"Girl I know you're tired of dealing with these fools. You can sleep with me," Markita told her.

"Ok but you're not into bitches or nothing like that right?" Jasmine doesn't play that funny shit.

"Girl I don't care about your sex. I don't give out pussy if you're not paying. Are you willing to pay?" Markita asked.

"Hell no," Jasmine frowns.

"Then you good. You're safer than a nun in this bitch," Markita assured her.

Dallas and the guys are laughing hard. Jasmine is a damn fool for asking that woman some shit like that. They all sat around talking, drinking, and playing cards. It is a good thing that they left the hotel. Her house feels more like home anyway. Might as well enjoy easy street because tomorrow some muthafuckas would lose their lives for sure.

Don Q, Tommy Gunz, and Big Nate entered the Rush Tower. Tammy his little dip had given them the key cards to the three rooms that Dallas and his team checked into. She didn't know that they aren't there anymore because they never checked out; they just left. Dallas had a feeling that the nigga had an inside scoop.

They took the stairs not wanting to chance someone hearing the elevator. The plan is to be in and out they carried guns with silencers on them. They were outside of the rooms each took a room to enter. Don Q went into the room and found no one at all. It doesn't even look like the room had been checked into.

Don Q made his way back to the hallway. Tommy Gunz and Big Nate came back his way. "What's good boy?

"Ain't no one been in these rooms," Tommy Gunz said.

"Damn that nigga knows that I'm laying on him. He shook the spot so he must have a layup bitch around here somewhere. I guess I have to wait for the nigga to come to me." Don Q isn't feeling that shit.

"Yeah how hard is the nigga coming when he comes to see you?" Big Nate asked. He is cool with Don Q but not enough to be risking his life in a war. He told that nigga too many times to tone that bragging shit down but he never listens. Now it is there to bite him in the ass.

"That I don't know just be at the office in the morning," Don Q told them.

They agreed on that, but Big Nate isn't planning on showing up. He has a wife and kids at home it isn't even his beef. Don Q is his boss, always rubbed his title in Nate's face, which caused Big Nate to lose respect for him. The nigga is green as hell, so he is not shocked that Dallas had him thinking they were friends. Don Q trusted Tommy Gunz with his life but the nigga is fucking Lola.

Don Q isn't cut out for that street shit. He was just smart when it came to numbers and money so a lot of low-level shit went on around him and he doesn't have a damn clue about it.

Chapter 32

The morning sun came through the living room window. Dallas rolled over knowing that it is time to face the music. He is ready to dance. Dallas knows that Don Q is waiting for his call, so it's time to oblige him. "What's real blood," Don Q answered as if he is still in Cali waving that flag.

"Damn you on that gang life at breakfast." Dallas laughs at his old ass.

"You always got to be ready family." Don Q sent him a subliminal message.

"I feel you on that I stay ready." Dallas let it be known.

"That's why I fuck with you, nigga." Don Q shook by Dallas's statement. He doesn't know how he got caught up in that shit, but there he is.

"So where I am meeting you because I'm trying to get this shit done?" Dallas asked.

"Man meet me at the Stallion. I know you remember where that's at from the last time you came here and took half of my bitches up out of there." Don Q was tight about that when it happened. That the nigga Dallas talked those whores into going back to the Lou with him to get some money pissed him off.

"Alright I will be there about an hour or so," Dallas told him ending the call.

Dallas went and woke up the crew. He gave them a few minutes to get it together. Markita was standing in the kitchen in a sexy red teddy that was hugging her body right. Dallas's dick got hard as hell. When she saw him come in the kitchen, she smiled at him. "Good morning sleepyhead. You want some breakfast?" she asked.

"If you're what I am eating." Dallas walked up behind her squeezing on her fat ass." He loved the way that muthafucka felt.

"Dallas are you about to pay to eat this pussy?" Markita asked dead serious.

He laughed. "Hell no girl!" Dallas backed up off her she must have bumped her fucking head somewhere.

"Ok then I suggest you get over there and get some of this bacon and eggs," Markita told him.

"That's fucked up," Dallas said as he made himself a plate.

"Is it? What's cold is when I met you I was looking for a boss to take care of me. Instead, you fucked me and told me that you aren't into keeping a bitch, and with a pussy, I could keep myself. Talked about me foul that I am giving up pussy to be left hungry with a wet ass. Then you gave me five hundred dollars because that's all it is worth to you," Markita reminded him.

Dallas is dying laughing because he did that. You had to be an ice-cold nigga to tell someone that. That shit takes him back to the bitch that he fucked and gave five dollars. Then he told her not to quit her day job because her pussy isn't about shit. "Damn you gonna use my teaching against me." He respected her hustle.

"Nigga hell after that day my pussy wasn't free no more." Markita hugged him. She loved that man and valued what he taught her. She knows bitches that have kids falling out the ass, living on low income, on section eight and broke, that keeps a wet ass. She is glad that Dallas opened her eyes, and if she ever stopped hoeing, she still isn't going to take a broke ass nigga to be her only nigga.

Zane, Dizzy, Mack, and Jasmine made their way to the kitchen. Mack isn't a morning person, and he is missing Tasha. "What the fuck is all laughing for?" Mack is grumpy. That is not okay for the people he was going to war with.

"Man shut the hell up," Zane told him.

"Man fuck you! Dallas why the fuck are we moving on this nigga so early? I thought we ran at night. This food cool but my wife's jams." Mack said taking a bite of the bacon.

"You ain't got to eat my shit, Mack." Markita doesn't play about her cooking.

"Girl don't trip off him. Tasha's just been spoiling that nigga. Brings him breakfast in bed while she naked," Jasmine said.

"See niggas talk too much how you know that?" Mack asked.

"My sister told me," Jasmine's talking ass said to him.

"Zane's bitch ass been telling my business." Mack chewed and talked.

"Aye, nigga I was trying to get my wife on that shit. She gonna tell me to make her breakfast in bed naked instead." Zane keeps it real.

The whole room busted out laughing. The knock on the door changed that. Markita reached in her kitchen drawer and grabbed her heat. What fucked her up is the fact the every muthafucka in the room has a gun on them at nine in the morning. She went to get the door. "Who is it?" she asked.

"Is Dallas here?" the female voice asked.

Markita opened the door because she knows the bitch has to know him to be asking for him by name. Jay is standing at the door. "Dallas here?" She didn't flinch at the woman holding a gun. That made Markita know that she had to be down with Dallas's team.

"Yeah he here." She let Jay in.

Jay walked in the kitchen, and Mack jumped up. "This what the fuck I'm talking about my dog here to cause hell." He loves Jay's swag.

"Who told you where we were?" Dallas asks everyone looked at Jasmine.

"What? Jay is mad.

"It doesn't matter anyway, she's here," Jasmine said and hugged Jay.

"If she gets hurt I'm blaming yo ass," Dallas told her.

"Yo ass," Mack cosigned.

Jasmine pushed him. "She won't!" She is going to have Jay covered.

"Well look, we have to move. I need all of you to park in the front and the back of that club.

Zane when you get the text "Deed," come in and handle business. Take out any muthafucka there. It's daytime, so we don't have a lot of time." Dallas put them up on the game plan.

Chapter 33

Don Q was sitting in his office when Lola came in the room with Nisha. He had her clean her up, so she doesn't look like he didn't take her word for it when she told him. He wanted to make it look like she has joined his team. Nisha is willing to go along with that because she doesn't want to be in that fucking backroom anymore.

She is looking as best she could, but they have to be a fool to think that Dallas wouldn't be able to tell that she had her ass whooped. Lola said that Dallas is there then she said, "For him to be on some bullshit he's here alone." Don Q looked at Nisha to see what she has to say about that.

"He's not alone. That's just how it looks but trust me, Y'all muthafuckas better be ready." Nisha looked around, and all she saw is Lola and Tommy Gunz. She knows that isn't going to be enough.

"Lola go out there and greet him. Tommy, I need you to guard the doors and be on the lookout for people coming in or around the place," Don Q told him wondering where the hell Big Nate's ass is. He had stopped by earlier to get some money out of the safe, but he hadn't seen that nigga since. If the nigga were smart, he would know that he wasn't going to see Big Nate anymore. Nate wasn't about to be a part of that shit. He has taken his family back to LA.

Lola walked out talking shit as always. Tommy wanted to act like the shit doesn't faze him, but he is shaken. Lola let Dallas in as Tommy stepped out the door. Dallas reached his hand out. "What's good potna?" Dallas's hand lingered as Tommy stared at it. "I understand I'm not a morning person either." He passed Tommy's bitch ass as he heard Lola say, "Right this way." Dallas shakes his head because she is the ugliest bitch he seen in his life, but he played nice.

"What's your name beautiful?" Knowing he lying she smiled.

"Lola Bandz." She is the first woman that he ever met the got uglier when she smiled.

"Bandz huh." Standing there looking like change.

"Yeah, baby. I am about that money." Dallas busted out laughing. He doesn't mean to, but he could no longer hold it. Dallas has to get his shit together. She looked like he is crazy as they enter the office.

Nisha is sitting there with her head down, and it caused Dallas to smile. There is no point in trying to rob the nigga. She has dimed him out just like he thought so now he is just going to take the shit.

"Don Q," Dallas spoke like he doesn't see Nisha.

"Lola guards the door," Don Q requested.

"Damn is it like that?" Dallas asked taking a seat.

"Yeah it is." Don Q for some dumb ass reason feels he has the upper hand knowing that Lola is standing at the door with the double-barrel shotgun.

"What's all this about?" Dallas leaned back in his chair. That pissed Don Q off because the nigga doesn't seem to shake at all. The nigga is sitting in his office bent back like that shotgun right behind his head meant nothing to him at all.

"Nisha would you like to tell Dallas what this was about?" She wished that he'd just taken her word for it and left her out of that shit.

"No!" She is scared as hell.

"I think that you should." Don Q gave her a cold look.

Dallas is over the bullshit. He is going to get what he came there for, but the plan had changed. He wanted all the shit the nigga has now. "Nisha hey baby long time no see. I didn't know that you were coming to Vegas. You could have saved your money and taken the jet up here with me. Can you tell me what this nigga so uptight about?" Don Q hates Dallas's smooth talking ass. He should have seen it coming.

"Look Dallas I just wanted out, and I know that you weren't gonna let me walk. Then Venom told you to kill me, so I had to do this to save my ass." Nisha knows that she has lost her damn mind fucking with Dallas.

"What is it that you had to do?" Dallas asked still laid back.

"I told him that you were planning to rob him for the deeds to his places. I know you think I'm wrong, but I'm not. I know that it was you that had that guy whoop my ass on that first mission. Then you were going to act like you were telling me what to do for my safety. I am not fucking safe with your ass." Nisha is pissed and on her feet talking shit like she is safe now.

Dallas can't believe that bitch has the nerve to sit there and talk that crap. He looked at Don Q. "So what now? You gonna kill me?" Dallas asked.

Don Q laughed, "You've got balls acting like you ain't within inches of your life." Don Q shakes his head.

"I am?" Dallas laughed.

"Yeah you are," Don Q assured him.

"What you waiting for then?" Dallas asked.

Don Q is fuming that nigga's ego is so fucking big it is unbelievable. Sitting here all smug and shit, he'd had enough of it. Nisha is glad that she is going to be there to see Dallas get what was coming to him. It served him right. Don Q thought he heard a boom, but he ignored it. Nisha wants to hide because she knows that the crew is coming for them. The damn office is a fucking shoebox. Nowhere to run and hide.

The only way in or out is the door that Lola is guarding.

Don Q reached for his gun and Dallas never budged. BOOM! Nisha's head is blasted across the wall. BOOM! Lola Bandz's face split like a watermelon. Don Q doesn't know what the hell is going on. All he knows is that the door flew open, and the two women that were in the room with him were dead.

Dizzy had a scope on Nisha through the window the office had. Mack is the one that moved in and took Lola's head off. Zane handled Tommy Gunz making sure the place is clear, as Mack has crept to the office to cause hell.

"Get the fuck up!" Dallas yelled at Don Q.

"Man, what the hell do you want from me? BOOM! Just like that, Don Q shot in the shoulder. "Uggghhhhhh aaaaaarrghhhhhhhhhhhh," he yelled falling back in his seat.

The phone began to ring. "Get it," Dallas ordered him.

"My arm's fucked up nigga," Don yelled "OOOOOOOOOOOOOhhhhhhhh grrrrrrrrrrrrrr." That four-five had his ass in pain.

"Get it muthafucka," Dallas yelled.

"Heeeelllllloooo grrrr." The pain has the nigga slobbering at the mouth.

"Donny," Don Q heard and knew that his shit has caught up to him.

"MOM!" Don Q forgot about the pain. He always lied about not having parents to make his struggle seem real. The truth is his parent had him in their fifties, God fearing people that were too old to stop him from the madness.

"Yes, baby these crazy women are here saying if you don't sign the deed of your businesses over. They are going to kill your father and me! What have you done to us," she cried.

Don Q has put them through so much, but this by far have to be the worst. "Mama hangs up can call the police. I will be dead by then, but you and daddy will be safe." He doesn't know who he is dealing with. If he doesn't think the two women will kill his folks he is wrong.

"Ok, I am going to call the police son. BOOM! Jasmine domed the daddy.

Don Q's mother screamed. "NOOOOOOOOOOOOO!" She dropped the phone, and Jay picked up the phone.

"Your father's dead would you like your mom to be next? Then we are heading to your baby mama's house if that doesn't matter to you.

"FUCK," Don Q yelled.

"That's right nigga, you fucked, signed the paper." Mack is ready to dome dude and sweeps the safe that is open and holding big cash.

"Go on and get that shit too Mack." Dallas sees him eyeing the money. Mack is on it filling the duffle bags.

"Alright! Alright! Alright!" Don Q is trying to think about what he could do. He has to save his mother but to sign all his shit over isn't something he wants to do. When he heard Jay start to count, "Ten, nine, eight…"

"Hold on lil mama I'm getting the shit out of the drawer." Don Q is leaking blood all over the papers.

He got the gun he has in the bottom drawer. Mack looked up, but he is too late. BOOM! Mack dead instantly. BOOM! So is Don Q's mother............

I WANT TO THANK EVERYONE AGAIN FOR TAKING THE TIME TO READ MY) STORY. AS I ALWAYS SAY READING IS FUNDAMENTAL SO KEEP READING. FEEL FREE TO CONTACT ME.